BRÜDERLEIN

To: Gary with so much
respect & thanks.

BRÜDERLEIN

Mr. Dee

VANTAGE PRESS
New York

This is a work of fiction. Any similarity between the names, characters, and places in this book and any persons, living or dead, is purely coincidental.

Cover design by Polly McQuillen

FIRST EDITION

All rights reserved, including the right of
reproduction in whole or in part in any form.

Copyright © 2004 by Mr. Dee

Published by Vantage Press, Inc.
419 Park Ave. South, New York, NY 10016

Manufactured in the United States of America
ISBN: 0-533-14824-3

Library of Congress Catalog Card No.: 2003099320

0 9 8 7 6 5 4 3 2 1

To the young and young at heart who thrill to the stories of the men who flew planes made of wood and canvas and fought in the skies of World War One

1

The morning mist had just begun to lift over the St. Pierre countryside. There was still a chill in the air. The birds still sang, despite the distant sound of the cannons at the front. Leftenant David Brooks stood outside his billet, sipping a cup of hot coffee laced with brandy. The sound of eight Sopwith Camels, being readied for the Dawn Patrol, drew his attention to plane number 8210. He remembered the first time he flew her. She was tricky to master and tended to pull to the right—yet, now the Camel had become a part of him and, like a pretty woman, he had grown to love her. She had gotten him out of many a tough battle.

"I say, Brooks, shall we have a go at it?" Myles Jeffries ventured. Captain Jeffries, the flight leader and a good friend to David, caused David to hand his unfinished cup to an orderly standing nearby as he nodded agreement to Myles.

Fastening his warm flight suit as he walked, David slapped Myles on his back and said, "Myles, old man, doesn't that handlebar mustache of yours ever get in the way?"

"Actually, old man, it scares the pants off the Huns' arses," he said, grinning as he left David and climbed into his Camel.

Having settled into his plane, David looked over toward Myles, who by now was checking with the rest of the flight to see if all was in order.

As Myles looked over at David, he gave him a thumbs up. With the flight ready, Myles raised his right hand above his head and brought it down sharply. The eight Camels raced across the still damp field and lifted off into the gray hazy sky. Myles led the flight up to eight thousand feet, leveled off, and set a course for the front. Their mission: to seek and destroy any surveillance planes trying to observe the British forces.

As they droned on, David took a quick glance at the new pilots. They were barely in their young twenties, full of excitement to take on the Huns. They had laughed a great deal that morning, but David knew the fear that squeezed their stomach muscles and the attempt they made to hide that fear.

I hope they make it through the day, David thought. Soon, the cold air and the smell of the petrol mixed with castor oil filled his nostrils and brought him back to the mission. Suddenly, James Aubrey spotted the small specks diving down toward them out of the clouds above. Jim bleeped his engine to alert the flight. Myles turned his flight up to meet the enemy head on, test firing their guns as he approached them.

As the Germans came into range, David noticed the lead Fokker was a new three-winged version known as the DRI. It was painted light blue with the face of an old mustached man on its nose.

In seconds, the sky was filled with the eighteen planes, twisting, turning, banking, diving, trying to get on each other's tail to fire a killing burst. In the trenches below, the infantry gazed skyward at the spectacle watching the life and death struggle above.

Myles banked hard, got behind a Pfalz, and started firing a long burst. David saw Myles' bullets stitch along the back of the Pfalz and reach into the cockpit of the hapless pilot. The German reared up as the Vickers pounded his body, then he slid down into his cockpit. The plane seemed to rear up and hang on its prop for just a moment, then it fell off on its right wing and started a long, spiraling turn to the zig-zag trenches below. David quickly banked to the left, and pulled back on his control column as he latched on to a Fokker DVII.

As he attacked the German, he spotted Connors' Camel spin around as flames began to lick back toward his cockpit. Rather than burn, Connors leaped and fell, his arms flailing in the air. This was his first mission.

David whipped his Camel around to get a shot at the Blue Fokker, but each attempt to line up his sights proved futile. He soon realized that the pilot was a master at his trade. The sound of bullets popping through canvas behind him caused David to throw his plane into a sharp diving turn to evade the enemy. As he leveled off, he found himself behind another lone Fokker. David opened up with both Vickers. He saw his tracers etch along the full length of the Hun's plane. Suddenly, the prop stopped turning. The hapless pilot looked back at David, as flames began to creep back toward the cockpit. The pilot rolled his plane over and fell free rather than burn in his seat.

David climbed back up near Myles and Aubrey. They noticed the Germans had reformed and were heading back to their field. The reason was soon apparent. A flight of French Spads, returning from a mission, spotted the fight and came in to assist.

Myles signaled for the flight to reform. As they did so, the French flight leader pulled alongside of Myles' plane, waved to him and gave Myles a thumbs up. Myles gave the Frenchman a smart salute in return.

Major Crawford, the C.O. of 131 Squadron, Royal Flying Corps, stood outside his office waiting for the flight to return. Out on the tarmac, the mechanics and plane handlers kept staring at the sky, waiting to greet their charges. They hoped against hope that the planes would not require many repairs.

The sound of the returning flight brought the field alive. The mechs ran out to receive their charges, the fire truck moved closer to the field perimeter. Myles was first to land, followed by the rest of the flight. David came in last as he waited for a new pilot to go around twice before he finally came in.

Major Crawford, seeing one plane missing, walked up to Myles to inquire what happened. The major turned and invited all the flight to the cantina for a pint of bitters. Myles and David eyed the other green pilots to see how they took the loss of a comrade.

Captain Edwards, second in command, joined them at the bar. Some of the flight stood there grabbing a few quick drinks and wiping the oil from their faces. As Crawford came into the cantina, Captain Edwards called everyone to attention. Smiling, the major put everyone at ease. "Gentlemen, the blue Fokker Triplane you saw today was flown by one of Germany's new top aces, Werner Foss. To counter this new threat to our front, Headquarters is moving Captain McCuddin and his 56 Squadron into our sector."

Cheers went up in the cantina at the mention of Captain McCuddin. Major Crawford continued, "This should cut our losses to a minimum. I was saddened at the loss of one of our young new pilots. He died fighting for King and country. I understand his remains are being brought here for burial with our fallen comrades. You will be notified when this is to take place.

"I've just received confirmation that our own Captain Jeffries and Leftenent Brooks each downed an enemy. Congratulations to you both!" As the major turned to look at Edwards, the captain called everyone to attention until the major had left the room.

David and Aubrey walked out together, but spoke very little. "See you later, Jim," David said as he walked off toward his billet.

David locked his door behind him as he entered his room. After removing his flight suit, he reached into his table and removed a bottle of whiskey. He took a long drink and sat down on the edge of his bed; then he took the picture of his parents from the small night stand and stared at it for a few moments. He loved them dearly for having given him a complete and happy childhood. David knew he was adopted, but somehow he had never pressed his parents for answers. *Some day, I must know about this half of a German Imperial Cross around my neck. What does it all stand for?* David put the picture back, took the bottle and poured himself another long drink. *One of these days soon, I must write Dad and ask him about all this.*

The Albatross DVa dropped low over the canvas hangar and touched down within a few feet of Hauptmann Kruger's office. The mechanics rushed over to grab the wing tips and put chocks under the wheels. Lieutenant Wilhelm Schroeder jumped down from the cockpit, pulling off his scarf and helmet as he approached the bewildered C.O. of Jasta 18.

"Willie, you'll be my demise yet," he said as Hauptmann Kruger put his arm under Willie's and offered, "Come, Willie! Have a schnapps and tell me how things are going at Schwerin. How did you find Tony Fokker?"

Otto Kruger led Willie into his office as Willie started to answer the many questions from Kruger.

"First Herr Hauptmann, he took me into a hangar where they were just finishing the installation of a new, more powerful Oberusal engine. Secondly, he showed me crates of new Clerget engines that the German government was able to obtain from Sweden. Tony was kind enough to let me take a new DRI up for a test flight with this new engine. I tell you, Otto, I was surprised; I was tempted to head for the front and take on the entire Allied air force!"

Hauptmann Kruger eyed Willie and smiled as he saw the excitement in Willie's face. "If it is as you say, Wilhelm, and we are able to get these new Fokker Dri deckers in quantity, we could help shorten this war and gain victory for the Fatherland."

"We will wait and see, Willie. By the way, you are dining with me tonight and an old friend from Fliegershule, Hauptmann Bruno Loerzer. He's getting to be quite an ace. I hear he has over thirty abshuss and has earned the Blue Max."

"Vielen dank, Herr Hauptmann, but first I must bathe and change into a uniform." Willie saluted the Hauptmann and left for his billet.

"Johann, you lazy lout, where are you?" Willie yelled jokingly.

"Here, here Herr Leutnant; I was polishing your boots," Johann answered.

"Thank you, my dear friend," Willie said. "When you are finished, Johann, could you please get out my good uniform? It seems I'm dining with the Hauptmann and a friend of his."

Johann prepared a hot bath for Willie. As Willie slipped into the soothing water, he lay back in the tub, soaking and letting his thoughts drift. *Ach, Liesel, my love, if only you were here with me now.*

The thought of her aroused him but Johann's voice asking if he needed more hot water soon shattered his concentration.

"Nein, danke, Johann; would you hand me the that towel, please?"

As Willie finished putting on his uniform, he reached into his drawer to get his watch. Looking into the drawer, he spotted the gold chain with half of a German Imperial Eagle on it. He picked it up, rubbing it fondly; and as he held it, he glanced at the picture of his mother on the desk. *Ach, Mutti, if only you were still here for me to come to.* Willie gently laid the coin back into the drawer.

"Here are your boots, Herr Leutnant," Johann said, kneeling down to help Willie put them on.

The dinner table was set with fine china and silver utensils which had been taken from a captured chateau. Two orderlies stood by to serve and cater to the needs of the Hauptmann and his guests. Hauptmann Kruger and Bruno Loerzer were chatting as Willie walked in.

"Bruno, this is Leutnant Wilhelm Schroeder whom I mentioned to you."

"Ah, yes, Wilhelm; Hauptmann Kruger speaks very highly of you."

"Vielen Dank, Herr Hauptmann," Willie said as Kruger motioned them toward the dining table.

After the dinner, with fresh cigars and good French wine,

Hauptmann Loerzer asked Willie how many planes he had shot down.

"Only nine, Herr Hauptmann," Willie answered modestly.

"Very good, Wilhelm," Bruno said as he patted Willie on the back. "If we keep this up, soon, there won't be any English dogs to shoot down." Willie looked over at Otto, but neither one smiled.

The slight drizzle and overcast weather added to the solemnity of Flight Officer Conners' funeral. His plane had been downed not far from Capy, just over the British lines. An infantry sergeant and two privates brought the charred remains to the field, where the sound of the drums beating half time march cadence accompanied the squadron to the cemetery.

Major Crawford gave a short eulogy, after which, the firing squad fired three volleys. Off in the distance, the bugler played a farewell song to a fallen comrade. As the mournful notes of the bugle rang out, David thought to himself, *How many more parades like this one, before this madness ends? Or will the time come, when they play this for me?*

Suddenly, David felt very old. *By God,* he thought, *March 7th I'll be twenty-five, an old man around here.*

David entered the cantina to the strains of "Here's to the last man who dies." Some of the men had gathered around the out-of-tune piano, singing with a drink in their hands, trying to drown their sorrows.

"I say, Brooks, rotten weather, what?" Myles said, greeting David and offering him a drink. "Connors was a fine chap," Myles continued as he raised his glass to salute his comrade's memory. "We shall all miss him."

David nodded agreement without looking up.

"They were all fine chaps, Myles, all fine chaps," David said, as he gulped down his drink.

"A rotten war, this, eh what?" Myles added as he too gulped down his double shot.

Major Crawford, standing in the corner talking to Edwards, observed David and Myles. "Captain, tonight I have to write the Connors family; I wonder how many more letters I will have to send to the families and loved ones?"

Crawford thought of the countless times he'd had to say, "They died for King and Country." Though he believed in both, the words were beginning to sound hollow. A courier brought Major Crawford an urgent message.

The sound of the arrival of new troops and new planes brought Hauptmann Kruger out of his office. The Albatross DVs were not what he had hoped for, but for the time being, they would have to do. Losses lately had been heavy and Otto was afraid that new fighter production could not keep up. He had hoped for some new Fokker DVIIs, or perhaps some of the new Triplanes that Willie had mentioned.

Willie, Anton, Emil and Hardy sauntered over to the cantina. Max Ehrlich, Otto's second in command, called everyone to attention as Otto walked in.

"At ease, gentlemen," Otto said, as he looked over the papers, then at the faces of the new young pilots standing before him.

"Gentlemen," he began. "You are now part of Jasta 18! This Jagdstaffel has so far been responsible for downing over eighty enemy aircraft, and these Abshusse would not be possible without the dedication and skill of our pilots! Their devotion to the Fatherland, their constant dedication to training and unselfish duty has made all of this possible.

"If you wish to survive this war, and to do your duty to the Fatherland, I suggest you listen and follow the lessons of our senior pilots. Take their every word to heart. My saddest duty is writing the parents and families of our gefallene. Please don't let me have to write your families.

"Lastly, gentlemen, I bid you welcome to Jasta 18. I wish you all, a long and happy association with us."

Max Ehrlich brought the men to attention; they remained that way until Hauptmann Kruger left the cantina.

Max ordered Willie, Anton, Hardy and Emil to report to Otto's office at once. As the four men headed for the office, Anton turned to Willie and said, "Willie, when do you think we will get the new Fokkers, or perhaps the new Triplane?"

"I wish I knew, Anton; these old Albatrosses can't maneuver like the British Camels. We need a better plane."

Willie began to knock on Otto's door, Otto's voice rang out, "Come!" as they entered, Otto looked up from his desk and motioned for the four to sit down. He stood up, reached into a cabinet and pulled out a bottle of wine and glasses. "Take a glass and help yourselves, please."

When everyone had settled down, Otto handed each man the records of one of the new pilots.

"Gentlemen," Otto said, "I hold each of your responsible for the training for each of these new men. I fully realize that flying missions two or three times a day, doesn't leave you time for training, but you have all witnessed the losses of those green pilots. Are there any questions?"

Anton rose slowly, looking first at his comrades, then at Hauptmann Kruger. He said, "Herr Hauptmann, I have been a member of this Staffel from its very founding. I, as I'm sure my comrades here, have watched these green men go to their premature deaths, not because of the prowess of the enemy, but because they lacked the most basic essentials to help them survive. May I suggest that we here be given some time to take these men up and teach them, before we send them out!" Anton, looking at the others, turned and sat down.

For what seemed like a very long time, Otto sat with his head down, deep in thought. Slowly he stood up, leaning on his fingers which were spread on his desk as he began to speak. "Each time we lose a man, a piece of me dies. I have asked you to do the impossible so many times, and you have never failed me. Now I ask you once again, to do this impossible task; keep flying your missions, and still find the time to train these new men. There are great battles yet to be fought, and we will need every capable man in the air. I will do all I can to get you the time to train them, but I must tell you, that time is running out. Thank you for coming, and good hunting."

After the talk by Otto, Willie and the others walked out and as they headed for their billets, Willie looked over at the four Albatrosses the replacements had brought in. Willie walked over to them, shaking his head as he examined them. Feldwebel Oster saw Willie's look of disdain and said to him, "They look as though they have seen many combat hours, Herr Leutnant. However, about this one, number 1215, a log shows that it just had a new engine installed, and seems to be in excellent condition."

Willie nodded and turned to go to his billet. As he did, Oster yelled after him, "I'll have your plane ready for dawn patrol, Herr Leutnant!"

Willie raised his hand in acknowledgment without looking back. He noticed from the plane's log, that it had been built at Schneidemuhl, outside of Munich. He remembered that Tony Fokker had told him they were now building the new Fokker DVIIs there. *I wonder,* Willie thought, *will we ever get the new planes?*

The morning was very busy as the mechanics hurried to get the planes ready for the first mission. Oster had already warmed up Willie's plane when Willie came out. Willie climbed into the cockpit as the engine idled and the mechanics held the tail section down.

As Willie sat there, he leaned forward to see if both ammunition boxes were full. Willie let the engine temperature come up, and advanced the throttle to six hundred rpm. Turning the magneto switch to both and with no major loss in rpms, Willie shoved the throttle up to 1300 rpms. Satisfied that everything was in order, Willie reduced his rpms as the mechanics pulled the chocks from under the wheels and spun the plane into the wind.

Willie looked over at the fledglings on either side of him. They both waved that they were ready. Willie raised his arm high and brought it down toward the direction of take off. As Willie gained altitude, he glanced back at the new men who were just pulling up behind him on either wing. Willie led the trio toward the Meuse River.

The trio droned on as Willie watched to see how well they held their positions. When they reached the Meuse River, Willie spotted the wreck of an old ship still sticking out of the water.

He signaled the two to hold their positions while he prepared for a strafing run. He shoved the plane's nose down and headed for the target. As he approached, he gave his Albatross a little right rudder and eased his nose up to line up on the target. Willie pressed both triggers and watched as his Spandau slugs kicked up the water just behind the ship, then smashed into the target kicking up wooden splinters along the entire target. Willie climbed rapidly, then leveled off in front of the new men.

Willie signaled Doerfler to make a pass. He slid off on his left wing, dropped his nose and headed for the target. He kicked his rudder both ways trying to line up on the wreck. As he neared the target, Doerfler opened fire. His shots were a little off but he managed to get a few into the ship.

When he rejoined Willie, he leveled off looking at Willie's face. Wilhelm smiled at Doerfler, nodded, then turned to his left and pointed to Fehler to try the same run. Fehler dropped his nose and headed for the wreck. As he approached the target, he seemed to hesitate, then came around for a second pass. Finally he came around and opened fire on the wreck. His shots went wild, and never came close to the target. *This one will need much practice,*

Willie thought. He turned them back toward Cambrai and their home base. They arrived just in time for dinner.

As Willie walked toward the dining room, Otto came along side and asked him, "Well, Wilhelm, how did they do?"

"Not bad for a first time out, but I think Leutnant Feiler will need much practice. By the way, Wilhelm, see me in my office when you're through here."

"Jawohl, Herr Hauptmann," Willie said, as they both entered the dining room.

"Sit down Wilhelm, try this wine, it's quite good," Otto offered. "Our troops at St. Quentin are going to attack the British positions there, to try and dislodge them. Our troops must secure a position near the Oise river in preparation for a much larger offensive. We have been ordered to provide aerial cover from enemy aircraft; also, we will have to increase our patrols, to try and stop any enemy observation around this area."

"Herr Hauptmann, will we have any help from some of the other Geschwaders?"

"Yes, we will, Willie, but at the same time, we don't want to tip our hand to the enemy."

"I want you to run this operation, Wilhelm. It won't be easy and I would prefer that this is not common knowledge among our Jasta."

"Who can I have work with me on this, Herr Hauptmann?" Willie asked.

"Pick anyone you like, but please impress on them, secrecy is most important now. But by the way, Wilhelm, some good news; Werner Foss and his Staffel have been moved to Douai, so you see, we will have the added support we need."

"That's wonderful news, Herr Hauptmann, it should make this effort a winning proposition. I think I would like to involve Hardy and Anton."

"Very good, Willie, but please, secrecy is of the utmost importance!"

"Zu Befehl, Herr Hauptmann"

As Willie turned to leave, he asked Otto, "Do you think we can leave the new men out of this effort?"

"You know the answer to that, Wilhelm, maximum effort means maximum effort."

Once Willie was outside the office, he shook his head as he walked away. Otto observed him through his window. "Someday, Wilhelm, you will have to make these same decisions, and my dear friend, I hope you will have the courage to make them."

2

The field was still damp from last night's downpour, as the lone SE5 with Squadron leaders' stripes on its wings came in for a perfect landing, water spewing back from its wheels. Major Crawford stood up, peering out of his office window, thinking *This has to be Captain McCuddin.*

The major walked out to the plane, as the mechs threw chocks under the wheels and helped Captain McCuddin out. The men in the cantina came out to look over the new Sopwith SE5 and to meet the famous Captain McCuddin, joined by Captain Edwards.

Major Crawford thanked the captain for coming on such short notice. "I say, Major, I haven't had a bite this morning and I—" Major Crawford interrupted the Captain. "Of course, Captain, it would be my pleasure."

Turning to Edwards, he asked him to have food sent over to his office. As the two walked toward Crawford's office, the Major flagged David, Jeffries and Aubrey to join them. David stopped long enough to tell one of the mechanics to be sure the captain's plane would be refueled and armed with ammunition.

After the food was devoured by Captain McCuddin, he laid his serviette on the table, leaned back and said to Major Crawford, "That's a fine chef you have here! I do believe ours came from some long forgotten brig." Everyone joined in the laughter.

Crawford had Edwards station two sentries outside the door, bade everyone to relax, brought out a box of cigars and offered everyone a cigar. The major brought out his pipe, puffing three times to make sure it was lit.

He settled back in the chair behind his desk, looked at Captain McCuddin and began.

"Gentlemen, Intelligence seems to feel the Jerries are planning a big push somewhere in the vicinity of St. Quentin. Three new squadrons have been moving into fields around Laon. They feel these squadrons are to support this pending attack." The Major turned to McCuddin and asked him to step up to a large map on the wall.

"My squadron will operate from Vert Gallent; we will fly as many missions as possible to thwart the Huns. I understand, from your major, that your Squadron will operate out of Bertangles. We will keep you apprised as to anything we find, as I'm sure, Major Crawford will keep me informed also. I wish you all, good hunting."

Captain McCuddin turned to Major Crawford, thanked him for the lunch and for a chance to meet the squadron. Captain Edwards stood up and reminded the flight leaders to pick up their area assignments.

As McCuddin stood up to leave, Captain Edwards called everyone to attention, as Major Crawford and Captain McCuddin walked out toward the captain's plane.

When McCuddin was strapped into his cockpit, he signaled the mechs to pull the chocks and, looking over to Major Crawford, he gave him a thumbs up and went racing down the field for a quick take off.

Major Crawford turned to return to his office, as the sound of the returning patrol reached his ears.

He scanned the sky until tiny specks became visible and they started to come in for a landing. The major counted the planes as they came over the field. A sigh of relief escaped his lips when he saw that all six had returned safely.

Major Crawford waved David over. "Be a good chap, get me the flight reports as soon as you can."

"Yes sir, Major," David said and started for Aubrey's plane which had just come to a stop.

"Well, Jim, how did it go?" David asked.

"Actually, very good old man, very quiet, no enemy aircraft in sight, but I think we should keep an eye near St. Quentin. How did the new men do today, James?"

"They were fine, but disappointed—no Huns in sight. Come Jim, I'll buy you a drink. Good to have you back! Take your flight over to the cantina; I'll see you there shortly."

David knocked on the office door and entered on hearing "Come," from Major Crawford's calming voice. As David came in, the major waved him to a chair without looking up. Leftenant Phelps, the line officer in charge, stood by the major's desk as he scanned the status report for all the planes.

"Well, Tom, how many planes can we put up tomorrow?" the major asked.

"Just now sir, we have fifteen Camels and three Pups, plus—if need be—I can work my crew and get another five planes by tomorrow morning."

"Tom," the major answered, "for the time being, we will need every available plane kept on ready alert, I know you and your crew will see to it."

"We will see to it, Major," Tom said. He saluted and left the office, giving David a nod as he passed him.

The major turned to David. "Sorry to keep you, Leftenant, but I had to finish with Tom first."

"No problem, Sir," David said, sitting down at the chair near the major's desk.

"Brooks, when we're through here, would you check with supply and see to it that we have ample fuel, ammunition, bombs and spare parts?"

"Yes, sir, I will," David answered.

"How did the patrol go? Did they encounter any enemy aircraft?"

"No, sir, Major, Jim said they did not encounter any Huns, but he did mention that there seemed to be some activity near St. Quentin."

"Hm, I'm not really surprised," the major said. "It seems, David, that our intelligence is fairly accurate. We'll have to alert all flights to pay particular attention to the area near St. Quentin.

"David, we got so caught up in this rotten mess, that we soon forget the amenities. Tell me, have you heard from your parents lately?"

"No, sir. As you know, Major Crawford, our mail has not arrived for some time."

"Ah yes, I'm glad you mentioned it, I'll call and find out what can be done to speed the mail delivery. It's so important for the morale of everyone.

"David," the major began, "Captain Edwards will be leaving us soon to report to High Command for a staff position. I shall miss him, of course, and with his departure, David, that leaves a Captain's position open here. I am going to recommend you, David; the men all respect you and since I have seen your natural leadership qualities, I can think of no one whom I would rather have in this most important position. What do you think?"

David was taken by complete surprise.

"Major, I'm at a loss for words, I just don't know what to say," David continued as the red in his face came back to normal.

"I am honored, sir, and I will certainly do my best, but I do have one question. Will I still be able to fly?"

"Of course! I still need you up there to help lead the squadron along with Myles." The smile returned to David's face. "Again, sir, thank you for your confidence in me."

Major Crawford stood up and walked from behind his desk to David.

"As you know, Brooks, Helen and I never had children, but if we had been so blessed, I would have been so proud to have had a son just like you."

"Thank you, sir, the shock still hasn't worn off, so thank you."

"No need, David, as soon as I receive the confirmation, I'll inform you. Good luck, Captain," the major said, as he slapped Brooks on the back and led him to the door.

The morning was a beehive of action, as Squadron 131 made ready to fight en masse. The sound of the engines running, the smell of the castrol oil and gas mixture filled the air. Major Crawford decided to lead the squadron for this battle. At his signal, six planes roared down the field and behind them another six, until the entire squadron was airborne and formed up, headed for the front.

Captain Jeffries led one flight, Brooks led a second flight with Jim Aubrey leading the third flight. Soon the front would come into view.

Hauptmann Kruger stood on the tarmac watching as his squadron lined up for take off. Willie looked back over his shoulder at Kruger, having first looked both right and left at the others waiting to take off. Hauptmann Kruger waved to Willie and nodded. Willie raised his arm and as he brought it down, the Staffel started taking off. As Wilhelm led his first flight up, the others immediately followed and by the time he reached 8000 feet, they were formed up and headed for the front.

As they neared the front, they could see the pockmarked earth below, the hundreds of miles of erupting ground as their artillery pounded the British lines. In the German trenches the men stood by their ladders, bayonets fixed, waiting for the barrage to lift, and the signal for them to climb out and advance toward the English trenches. Those old timers who still survived many such attacks thought: *How many more can I come back from alive?* The new young men stood by their ladders, the fright sticking out on them like acne pimples on a teenager.

As soon as the barrage lifted, Willie watched as Foss and his Staffel dove down and began to machine gun the British trenches. Willie watched as he saw the English soldiers twisting and falling from the withering fire. Suddenly, he saw a Pfalz rear up and crash into No Man's Land. One second later he saw a Fokker trying to climb as fire licked back toward its cockpit. Willie suddenly realized that enemy fighters were here. He signaled his flight and they began to dive toward the trenches and the many enemy planes that had suddenly appeared.

Willie spotted a Sopwith Camel, pulled in behind him, and fired a long burst. The pilot whipped his Camel up in a sharp turn, banked to the left to try and get behind Willie. Willie turned into him and as he did, his sights crossed the Camel for a moment. He fired a long burst, saw the plane waver, then twist and begin its dive to the hell below. As it fell, flames began to lick back toward the hapless pilot.

Willie's flight split off and jumped into the fight. As they twisted and turned trying to find any enemy and trying to stay out of harm's way, Willie saw Foss's blue DRI sit on the tail of a Camel, fire a long burst and saw the pilot of the Camel rear up then slip into his cockpit as the Camel made its final plunge to the war-torn earth below.

Willie spotted a French Spad and, banking hard to the right, pushing his nose down, correcting his sights with his rudder, he started to open fire.

As he sat hunched over his sights, Willie suddenly felt the *tac-tac-tac* of holes being punched into the back of his plane. Willie broke off his attack, shoved his nose down steeply then glanced back at his attacker. Before he had a chance to evade the enemy, the *tac-tac-tac* began to pound his engine section. Smoke suddenly poured out from his engine, his controls were not responding as they should.

Willie dove for the earth, trying to slip to the right to keep the flames from licking back to his cockpit.

Spotting a clearing on the German side of the lines, Willie headed for it as the flames grew closer and closer. Willie flattened his dive, leveling off, and started to attempt a landing. When his wheels touched the grassy knoll, Willie cut his engine. Suddenly, he hit a deep rut, as his Fokker nosed over. As he tried to unbuckle his safety belt and drop out of his plane, he felt a stabbing pain in his leg.

Men from a nearby artillery position, ran over, freed Willie and pulled him away from the fiery wreck just as it exploded.

As they laid Willie on the stretcher, Willie glanced up hearing the roar of a Camel buzzing overhead. Willie noticed an American flag painted on its side. The pilot looked at Willie, gave him a quick salute and climbed to get back into the fight.

Major Crawford was first to land. He climbed out of his Camel, nodding to a mechanic that the plane was fine, and headed toward the hangar. As he walked, he kept looking over his shoulder, watching each plane land, but feeling a pang in his heart, knowing that three Camels had been lost.

He walked over to Phelps in the hangar and told him to check each plane carefully, sure that many would have bullet holes in them. Satisfied that he had touched bases with Leftenant Phelps, he headed for the cantina where he knew the men would be congregating.

As the major entered the cantina, he spotted Jeffries and Aubrey next to the bar. "Did any of you chaps see what happened to Garon, Manson and Newbourgh?"

"I saw Newbourgh buy it, sir," Aubrey said. "It was that damned blue triplane. I tried to get in a shot but I never was able to draw a bead on him."

Myles told the major that he had seen Garon and Manson get hit, but was too busy with a Hun to see what happened.

"By the way, Major," Myles said, "I did see Brooks and

Aubrey each get a DVII. I couldn't help seeing Brooks, here, follow that Hun right down to the deck, then buzz him."

"Well done, both of you, but I need not remind you that in a fight, we don't take time to see if they crash, we go after the next one. Let's see now," the Major continued. "That makes ten for you, David, eight for you, Myles, and five for you, James. Well done to all of you. Splendid."

As the Major headed for the door, he motioned to David to follow him.

Once outside, Crawford turned to David. "That Foss fellow is real trouble; I hope someone can put him away soon!"

"Well, sir," David added, "At least we have Captain McCuddin close by, it would be something to watch if the two ever met in combat."

"My dear Leftenant Brooks," the major added, "The days of jousting knights are long past. This is a rotten war at its best."

Willie lay on the stretcher, staring up at the sky, waiting for an ambulance to take him to a front line hospital. Up above he watched the life and death struggle going on. Some of the planes turned and banked; smoke poured out as they started their final death plunge. He could hear the rat-tat-tat of the machine gun fire. The thought of never being up there again began to bother him, as the ambulance pulled up and four soldiers lifted him into its open doors. As they locked his stretcher in, he felt a stabbing pain in his leg. Before they closed the doors, a corpsman reached in, handed him a bottle of schnapps and said, "Here, Herr Lieutenant—take a good mouthful, it will help ease the pain."

"Vielen Dank, Herr Feldwebel, ich hoffe, ich hoffe."

Willie lay back on the stretcher, trying to prepare himself for the bumpy ride to the hospital. He looked over at the soldier lying on the other stretcher. Willie tried to start up a conversation with him, but there was no answer. He suddenly realized that the man was dead. *Well,* Willie thought, *at least for him, the hell of the trenches is over.*

As Willie thought about having being shot down, he said to himself. "I must meet that plane one day! Hm, I wonder why an American flag? Must be a Yankee who joined the English."

As he started to doze off slightly, Willie thought, *I must admit he's a gentleman; he could have machined us but instead flew down to see if I survived, then saluted me. Must be an aristocrat.* As the ride dragged on, Willie kept looking at the dead soldier and wondered about his family. Did he have children, perhaps? *Ach,* he thought, *it's this rotten war.*

"Leutnant," the hospital orderly said quietly, "Forgive me, sir, but it is time for your bath and to change the bandages." Willie stared at the attendant suddenly bewildered at the unfamiliar surroundings as he looked around the room.

"Where am I? What is this place?" Willie said, still trying to understand what was happening. The sound of another voice caused Willie to look toward the door of his room. "I'm your Doctor, Leutnant. My name is Major Reis, I'm chief surgeon here. This is Marionburg, and you are in the military hospital here. Apparently, you had so much pain that the field doctor gave you a strong sedative. They tell me you have been sleeping for three days now."

"What seems to be my problem, Herr Doktor?"

"First Leutnant Schroeder, you have a compound fractured leg. Secondly, you were hit by a bullet which, fortunately for you, went right through your leg and it was a clean wound."

Willie winced at the prognosis. "Tell me, Herr Doktor, will I still be able to fly?"

"Of course, Leutnant. However, you must allow your leg to heal. You're young yet, it should be as good as new in about four to five weeks."

As Dr. Reis started for the door, he stopped and turned toward Willie. "By the way, Herr Leutnant, it seems you are to recuperate at a place called Oberschliesheim." Smiling, the Doctor looked at Willie and said, "I understand you have a pretty young nurse there—at least that's what Hauptmann Kruger said when I called him to report your being here." Willie turned red as some of the nurses standing nearby, overhearing the Doctor, giggled and smiled at Willie.

"You should be able to leave in a few days, Herr Leutnant. I'll be in to see you before you go."

"Vielen Dank, Herr Major," Willie said as the Major left the room.

As Willie lay back down on the pillow, he thought, *Ach, that Otto, he talks too much, but he is my dear friend. I must remember to thank him when I next see him.*

The thought of seeing Liesel filled his mind.

Oberst Johann Von Ritter strode into Hauptmann Kruger's office. Oberleutnant Ehrlich, spotting him, called out, "Achtung," bringing everyone to attention. Von Ritter smiled, putting everyone at ease as he walked up to Otto to shake his hand.

"Otto, my dear friend, I'm sorry I did not notify you of my coming. I'm on my way to see Werner Foss and since his Staffel is not very far from here, I said to myself, this is a good time to see my dear friend Otto!"

The Colonel looked at the others in the room. As they left, they each turned, saluted the Oberst and went out.

"Otto, this long ride has made me quite dry. Would you by any chance . . . "

Otto interrupted the Colonel and with much fluster, said, "Of course, my dear friend," as he brought out a bottle of his best French wine and two glasses. Otto handed the Oberst a glass; touching the Colonel's glass, Otto said, "Prost." Von Ritter returned the toast with, "To our Fatherland and to old friends."

The Colonel eased into a chair as Otto sat down behind his

desk. As the Oberst began to talk, Otto refilled the Colonel's glass and pushed the bottle toward him.

"As you know, Otto, I'm being moved up to General Schmoelz's office as an aide to the General. Since he knew I was coming this way, he asked me to give you some good news. First, Otto, your request to elevate Leutnant Schroeder to Oberleutnant, has been approved."

"Could you have him come here? I would like to personally present him with his promotion."

"I'm sorry, Johann; he was shot down, wounded, and is recovering until his leg heals."

"Ach, I'm sorry to hear this, Otto; I do hope he will be back with you soon."

"Herr Oberst, I will see that he is notified at once; I know how pleased he will be.

"He is a fine officer, a credit to the Corps and is highly respected by the entire Jasta," Otto said, looking to see the Colonel's response.

"So I have been given to understand, my dear Otto. Some day, perhaps, he may have a Staffel of his own."

Otto was elated at the thought. Willie was like a son to him and he wanted to see him advance.

"You know, Otto," the Oberst continued, "the General is very aware of your splendid leadership. I think someday something good will come your way; until next time, keep up the good work and let us hope soon the Fatherland will win this terrible war."

Otto led the Oberst outside. The Colonel leaned back in his open staff car, smiled at Otto and wished him, "Halse und Bein Bruch," as his car sped away.

April, 1917, would be remembered by the Allied Air Services as "Bloody April." The Allied losses were staggering. By September, with so much rain, the fields had become very soggy. Visibility was poor and aerial observation was at its lowest. For the men in the trenches, the slaughter had not abated; the mud, the rats, the inability to even bury the dead had left the infantry in a terrible state of mind.

September 23rd, the weather began to lift, the sun peeked through the clouds, and for the pilots, it meant that the time to go aloft had once more returned. On every airdrome, the planes were rolled out of their canvas hangars, fueled, armed, and made ready for the business of war.

Werner Foss, one of Germany's greatest aces, was up early that morning. He was eager for the hunt for Allied planes. He stood by his blue Fokker DRI triplane, checking every last detail as he made ready to fly a lone patrol, which he often did.

At Vert Gallant, Captain McCuddin and his flight were already racing down the field for a patrol. They rose rapidly and headed for the front.

Captain McCuddin pushed his flight to the highest operating altitude to gain an advantage.

Looking over both sides of his plane, he suddenly spotted a lone blue Fokker DRI flying below. McCuddin signaled the other four SE5s in his flight to attack this lone Fokker, which was flying along, seemingly unaware of any other planes in the sky. As Captain McCuddin looked down at the Fokker DRI, he thought to himself, *This has to be an easy kill.* He signaled the other four men in his flight and down they dove to finish off this lone blue Fokker triplane.

Werner Foss spotted the five and turned his DRI upward into their path to meet them head on. As McCuddin's men came into range, Foss opened fire, putting holes in two of the British SE5s. The five broke up and started trying to down the lone Hun. Foss whipped his Fokker around, putting holes in all five of the English planes. A flight of six Albatross scouts, returning from a mission, spotted the battle and attempted to intercept to aid their comrade. However, a flight of French Spads saw the melee and joined the fight, chasing the Albatrosses away.

By this time, Foss, who had been dishing out the punishment, began to take quite a few hits himself. To get away from McCuddin's guns, Foss dived for the deck. As he neared the ground, he leveled off. Then, suddenly, his plane nosed into the ground and exploded. . . . Leutnant Werner Foss, one of Germany's greatest aces, was dead at age twenty.

The news of Foss's passing reached all the Allied airmen who had raised toasts to his honor. The men of 131 Squadron stood around the cantina drinking and discussing Foss's feats as Captain Edwards walked in and reminded the men, that there was still a war on.

"Gentlemen," he said, "your flight schedules have been posted, I suggest you look at them and be prepared for tomorrow."

Major Crawford called Jeffries, Brooks and Aubrey into his office and told them the good news. They were to receive three new Sopwith Snipes, fitted with 230 HP Bentley engines.

"I understand they can climb to 6500 feet in five minutes. Farnsworth believes they can out fly anything the Huns have. Also, gentlemen, I would like each of you three to take one, test it and let me know what you think."

Major Crawford looked into the faces of each of them as he spoke. "In addition," he continued, "we're getting three new Sopwith TF2-type aircraft with their crews. I have been told they have armor plate around the crew area and the petrol tank. They are designed for low level attack; they are two-seaters and heavily armed." As the major finished speaking, a cheer went up in the room from all the men.

"I say, Major," Jeffries spoke up, "am I to assume there is something in the wind to go along with this new land fall?"

"Captain Jeffries, when the time comes, I will certainly apprise you of the situation. In the meantime, let's keep on shooting down those Jerries!"

Major Crawford brought out two bottles of good French wine. The men left after all the wine was gone, the war forgotten for a short time as they strode back to their billets.

3

As the train pulled into the Hauptbahnof in Munich, Willie looked out of the curtains in his compartment. He noticed the unruly crowds, the people begging, he saw the anger in so many faces. *What in God's name is going on here?* A wounded infantryman, getting off the train with Willie, saw the look on Willie's face.

"Leutnant, they are hungry; too many men will not be coming back and for so many of them, the war is lost."

Willie looked over at the sergeant, "The war is far from over, my friend. When we are victorious, this will all be forgotten."

"For us, Herr Leutnant, at least it is over for a short while." Willie smiled at the soldier and waved goodbye to him as he hobbled away.

"Willie, Willie! Liebschen! Over here." Willie spun around to see Liesel running to him. Willie dropped a crutch as he grabbed her with one arm, holding her tight and kissing her for the longest time.

"Come, my darling! The car is over here." As she led the way, Eric, the chauffeur, picked up Willie's suitcases and put them into the trunk. He then helped Willie into the car. Liesel took blankets to cover his legs as she cuddled up to Willie for the long ride back to Oberschliesheim. As the car started to pull away, Liesel seeing Willie looking out at the people in the streets, pulled down the small shade and took Willie in her arms . . .

"Leutnant Schroeder, you are home, dear," Liesel said as she gently woke him. Willie rubbed his eyes, and realizing where he was, he handed the crutches to Liesel as Eric reached in and helped him out of the car.

As Willie maneuvered the crutches back under his arms, he stared at the Eck mansion and thought, *I don't recall it being so large.*

Frau Eck came over to Willie, kissed his cheek and said, "Herr Schroeder, it has been such a long time, much too long. Wilkommen, come! You must be tired and hungry. Eric, be good enough to take the Leutnant's things to the guest room and tell Franz I wish to see him."

Franz appeared suddenly with a wheelchair and pushed it into the house.

The Eck estate was vast and covered many acres that had, at one time, belonged to Maximillian, brother of Franz Joseph of Austria. The beautiful lawns were manicured and the flowers filled the air with their scent. The leaves on the trees were turning shades of reds and golds.

Liesel thanked Franz for bringing out the wheelchair, Liesel pushed Willie into the spacious living room. Frau Eck summoned the butler and told him to bring refreshments. As Willie sat there waiting, he gazed at the large paintings on the walls. Most of the portraits were of dead family members. The men were decked out in full military regalia. Many wore spiked helmets, some with plumes adorning them. Every face was stern as befitted a Prussian officer of that time.

Off to the side were the gun cases and, on the wall, antlers of deer shot on the hunt.

"How is Herr Eck?" Willie asked Frau Eck.

"He is well, thank you, Wilhelm. He is a General now and stationed in Ulm, but just now, he is on duty in Munich. There is so much unrest there, Walther has been sent there to quiet the agitators. The General seems to feel that most of the problem is with the Communists."

"Gruss Gott, Herr Schroeder!" A young voice rang out.

Young Walther ran up to Willie and kissed him on the cheek. "We have been following your exploits, haven't we, Mutti?"

Willie grinned at Walther and, pushing him back to get a better look, he said, "Let's see, now—Waldy, you must be about fourteen by now?"

"Nein, I'm sixteen now and soon hope to become a pilot like you."

Frau Eck cut Waldy short with a mild reprimand and told him to address Willie as "Herr Leutnant."

After the refreshments and having caught up on the amenities, Liesel said to Willie, "Come, Liebschen, let me help you to your room."

Willie sat on the soft mattress, trying to remember when he last sat on such a soft bed. Franz gave a polite knock and when invited in, brought Willie's suit cases into the room.

"Excuse me, Herr Leutnant, I will come back later and unpack for you."

"Vielen dank, Franz," Willie said as Franz closed the door behind him.

Liesel took a quick look down the long hall, then, down the staircase and hurried back into Willie's room. "Oh, how I've missed you, darling!" she said as she bent over to kiss Willie who was sitting on the edge of the bed. He quickly pulled Liesel down on the bed and started to roll over on top of her. She gently pushed Willie off. Shaking her finger at him she said, "Your leg, darling! You must be so careful."

"It's not my leg I'm thinking about just now, my love," Willie said, grinning from ear to ear.

"You are still a naughty boy," Liesel said coyly. They were both startled by the knock on the door.

"It is Franz. May I come in?"

"Come," Willie said.

"Bitte, Herr Leutnant, may I unpack your things for you?"

"Yes, of course," Willie said, as Liesel turned toward the windows to keep Franz from seeing her red face.

"Willie, dear, this is Franz, he will help you in every way."

"It will be a pleasure for me, Herr Leutnant," Franz added.

Liesel left the room as Franz began to unpack Willie's luggage. "Tell me, Franz, how long have you been with Eck family?"

"For a very long time now, Herr Leutnant. Liesellotte was just two years old when I came here.

"Excuse me, Herr Leutnant, would you like to take a warm bath?"

"Yes, thank you, Franz, that would be nice."

As Liesel came down the stairs, Frau Eck noticed some tears in her eyes. "Did you and Wilhelm have words, dear?"

"Nein, Mutti, we still love each other, but he seems so different. He seems to have aged so fast, he does not laugh like he used to."

"Ach, my dear daughter, sometimes I think you are still a little girl. Don't you realize what he has been through? How many of his comrades he has seen killed, and how many other young men he has had to kill? Be patient dear, one day this terrible war will end; Wilhelm will come home for good and you both will have many beautiful children."

Liesel smiled at her mother, hugged her and kissed her cheek. "You are so wise, Mutti, and I am so childish."

"Wash your face now, Liebschen; we don't want Wilhelm to see tears."

Frau Eck watched Liesel walk away and thought, *This terrible, terrible war.*

Willie stood by the mirror, leaning on one crutch, as he finished buttoning up his tunic and arranging his medals. The sound of a large car pulling into the driveway drew his attention.

Willie looked out of the large window at the car below as a tall, gaunt man stepped out of the back seat, the door being held open by a soldier in field gray uniform. The officer said a few words to the soldier, who then saluted the general, got back into the car and drove away.

General Gerhardt Von Eck entered the already opened door and gave Frau Eck a polite kiss on her cheek as Franz stood by to help the general remove his coat. The sound of Willie's crutches hobbling down the stairs, caused the general to look up and as he saw Willie he said, "Ach, Wilhelm, it has been a long time, how do you feel?"

"I'm doing much better, Herr General. It's good to see you again, sir. I hope I won't be a bother to you and Frau Eck, sir."

"Nonsense, Wilhelm, you are always welcome here."

The general slid his hand under Willie's arm and led him to an easy chair in the spacious study.

Handing Willie a glass of brandy, the general sat down next to him and said, "Tell me, Wilhelm, does your wound hurt very much? I have a doctor nearby if you should need one."

"Nein, Herr General, it does not pain me that much. Hopefully, it should mend soon and I can get back to my Staffel."

"Said like a true German officer, Wilhelm! We are very proud of you."

Frau Eck interrupted the conversation by inviting them to come sit down to dinner. The dining table was immense, large enough to seat at least twenty people. It was set with a beautiful damask table cloth, gold candle holders, Meissner and Rosenthal china. General Eck sat at the head of the table, Liesel on his right and Willie on his left. Frau Eck sat at the far end with Walther. The servants ran in and out of the kitchen, bringing food and removing dirty dishes.

The dinner took over two hours, with some light talk and pleasantries. As they ate quietly, the General and Willie discussed the war.

The General stood up, came around to Willie and helped him up. "Come, Wilhelm, we'll leave the ladies to their wiles and we'll have a cigar and brandy in the study."

Willie gazed over at the gun cases with so many fine rifles and the many hunting trophies hanging on the wall. The General offered Willie his choice from a box of cigars as he sat down next to Willie, a light at the ready.

"Tell me, Wilhelm, how are your parents?"

"Fine, Herr General, thank you."

"I know how proud your parents would have been of you!"

"Yes, Herr General, but the Schroeders have been like my parents, they always treated me as their own."

"I understand that Herr Schroeder is titled but never uses his Von; but be that as it may—here, Wilhelm, have another brandy. By the way, Wilhelm, we have a flying school near by, I'll tell Lieselotte to take you over there for a visit. I'm sure the fledgling pilots would like to meet a real hero."

"Thank you, Herr General, but at this moment, I don't feel like a hero."

"Nonsense, Wilhelm! You are too modest."

"Tell me, Herr General, when I arrived at the Hauptbahnohof in Munich, I saw quite a disturbance, some rioting, much unrest. What is happening?"

"You may not be aware, Wilhelm, but the war has drained most of our food supplies. The people are hungry, many of our brave men will not return and the people have lost their national pride. What you saw, was mostly agitators, Communists and trouble makers. When we are victorious, Wilhelm, it will all be forgotten."

A light knock on the door interrupted the conversation. "Please, Father, may I have some time with our honored guest?"

Herr Eck smiled at his daughter. "Of course, my dear."

As the general stood up, he turned to Willie and said, "We shall have many hours to talk, Wilhelm. Liesel, take good care of our guest." The General kissed Liesel's cheek.

As General Von Eck closed the doors behind him, Liesel kneeled down in front of Willie, kissed him and said, "I love you so much, darling, I wish you didn't have to go back. I'm sure Father could arrange it so that you could stay here."

Willie was caught off guard. He gently pushed Liesel away. "Liesel," Willie said with a stern look crossing his face, "flying is my life! I could never forgive myself, if I did not give our Fatherland all that I can."

Liesel paled as she apologized to Willie. "It's just that I love you so, and I want you with me. Is that so wrong?"

She looked away so that Willie could not see the tears beginning to fill her eyes. Willie stood up. Leaning on one crutch, he took out his handkerchief and gently wiped Liesel's eyes. "When this terrible war is over, my darling, I'll come back, and we will raise many beautiful little Liesels together." She smiled a sigh of relief as Willie said, "Come, Liebschen, we must join the others." Liesel put her arm around Willie to help him out.

Frau Eck walked up to Willie and kissed him on his cheek as she handed him a beautiful cane with a gold handle carved into the Imperial Eagle.

"My husband and I would love you to take this, Wilhelm. It belonged to my husband's great uncle. He was a famous Oberst in the Uhlans during the Franco-Prussian War; his picture is that one next to my great grandfather."

"I don't know how to thank you. Frau Eck, you have all been so kind."

The general walked over to Willie, and putting his arm on Willie's shoulder, he said, "After all, Wilhelm, you are like family to us. I hope soon, you will not have need of such things. Come, my boy, sit down and have a good cigar with me; Franz, bring us the brandy please!"

Willie sat looking at the cane, rubbing its grip and smiling at both Herr and Frau Eck . . .

With America now fully in the war, the tide was beginning to turn in favor of the Allies, although trench warfare sapped the lives of thousands of infantry on all sides. The invention of the machine gun, the tank and poison gas all added to increase the death toll and misery that war brings.

The men in the trenches were getting used to seeing the dueling of the knights of the air, watching the planes as they fell into the muddy No Man's Land below. As they watched, it was always with the same feeling. *At least the lads don't have to live with the bloody rats and the stench of death around them.*

November 2nd, 1917: the combined Allied command ordered an all-out offensive on a thirty-mile front from Lille to Douai, hoping to penetrate what they felt was a weak section of the German lines. They were planning to use the greatest number of tanks ever used to protect the attacking infantry. Air units from Cachy and Bertangles would be moved to the field at St. Pol; French units from Spa 19 would also be part of the offensive.

Major Crawford dispatched Captain Jeffries, Leftenants Brooks, Aubrey and eight other pilots to St. Pol as his contribution to this effort. The eight planes from Bertangles were the first to land at St. Pol. Other aircraft began to come in right behind them, causing mechanics and plane handlers to race around trying to spot them in proper locations.

Ack-ack units soon were seen around the entire perimeter of the vast field.

Myles and all the pilots from Squadron 131 had already gathered at the large bar, getting acquainted with the incoming pilots and putting away a few drinks. Once all the men had arrived, and with the many staff cars now visible, a meeting was called at a large, hastily set up tent. The blare of a loud speaker, ordered all personnel to report to the tent.

The hastily rigged large tent, was soon filled with the noise of pilots and staff officers. "Attention!" was yelled by the St. Pol commandant as everyone stood up at attention. He was followed in by a high ranking general and two of his staff officers.

The C.O. of St. Pol told everyone to be seated, "Gentlemen," he began his introduction, "this is General Goodall. I suggest you pay attention because the outcome of this operation will ultimately fall on your shoulders." He turned to the General who stood up, walked over to a large map and then turned to face the men.

"Very soon the entire front, as indicated on this map, will open up with the sound of over eight hundred guns. This will herald the beginning of our major offensive. Our Intelligence tells us the Germans have moved added squadrons into their fields in this sector. This confirms for us, that the Huns must have some idea what we are up to. This is the reason that we have built up our forces here and at surrounding air fields. Our French Allies, who are a part of this effort, have also doubled their numbers at the nearby air fields.

"With the enemy aware, we expect some casualties, but we hope to keep them to a minimum. Our ground forces will bear the brunt of this action and I needn't tell you what this will be like for them. Our function will be first, to prevent enemy aircraft from hindering our ground forces; secondly, your mission will be to strafe and bomb the enemy to such a degree, so as to enable our forces to unseat the Germans with the least amount of casualties.

"We must succeed! If we do, this could be the beginning of the end for the Germans, and hopefully, the end to this terrible war!"

The General handed his pointer back to the C.O. of St. Pol. Once again, he called out, "Attention!" as everyone stood up.

"May God save the King and England."

Myles told the men of 131 Squadron to follow him to his billet. As they left, the pilots headed to their individual units for final instructions.

"Remember, we will be up against some of the Jerries' best men. Stick as close as you can to your leaders." As the men stood up to leave, Myles showed them thumbs up and said, "Let's have a go at it!"

Brooks and Aubrey walked up to Myles' plane, as he sat in it pulling on his helmet. "Tally ho, old man," Aubrey told Myles and slapped him on his back. The sound of the planes' engines was deafening, the smell of castor oil and gas mixture filled the air and nostrils.

David was strapped into his new Sopwith Snipe. A freshly painted American flag glistened on its side. He looked both to the right and left at the other eight Camels, satisfied that they were ready, he raised his arm and brought it down sharply. All nine planes of David's flight raced down the field and lifted off into the patchy sky. David looked back over his shoulder, his flight raced to catch up with him and fall into their respective positions. As the two Vee formations droned on, David pulled his fur-collared jacket up closer around his neck to keep out the bitter cold air. He felt the exhilaration of the power in his new Snipe.

David leveled off at six thousand feet. One thousand feet above him and off to the right, Aubrey's flight held its assigned position. Finally, David looked up and spotted Myles' flight taking the high cover. They flew on, staring at the sky in all directions, looking for Huns. As they neared the front lines, David could see the zig-zag slits of the trenches, the yellow bursts of the barrage tearing up the already torn earth below. He could see large, lumbering tanks moving slowly toward the German positions.

He spotted the TF2 low-level attack planes doing their work. The gray clad troops toppled over from their withering fire. Germans were falling like new-mown wheat. David looked to his left and saw Aubrey's flight diving toward the trenches below. Seeing a large group of Fokkers and Albatrosses trying to knock out the ground attack planes, David took one last look above and around him and signaled his flight to hold their positions. Suddenly the sound of plinking, through the aft end of his plane, snapped David into near panic.

A group of Fokkers had slipped in from the sun and caught him off guard. The flight group saw the Huns and were soon tangling with them. The sky was filled with turning, diving planes, each one trying to get on the tail of an enemy. David put his Snipe into an Immelmann turn; he came around, shoved his nose down and sat on the tail of the Fokker. He caught the Fokker in his sights and fired a long burst into the enemy cockpit.

The German pilot reared up in his cockpit and slid back down, as the plane flipped over and started its final dive into No Man's Land below.

As David swung around to find another Hun, he saw an Albatross, trying to avoid a Camel on its tail, slam into a second Camel. Both planes erupted into a fiery explosion. Pieces of steel filled the sky. The pilot from the British plane jumped clear rather than be burned alive.

The thumping of his rudder caused Brooks to whip his Snipe around in a tight turn and shove his nose down. As he dived to get out of the line of fire, he glanced back over his shoulder, and saw the attacking Fokker suddenly flatten out. David pulled out of his dive, came up under the Fokker and raked the DVII from nose to tail.

David pulled up behind the Fokker, ready to fire again, but saw smoke beginning to pour out from under the Fokker's engine. For just a second, Brooks pulled alongside the crippled Fokker. The German pilot looked over at Brooks, saluted him, and, to David's amazement, he climbed out of his stricken plane and jumped. The German pulled his rip cord as his parachute blossomed out and he started to float down to the earth below. The sight of the French Spads joining the fight, was heaven-sent to David. He signaled to form up for the flight back to St. Pol.

As each plane came into position, David realized that two were missing. Brooks took one last look at the trenches as he headed his flight for St. Pol. He could see the Tommies climbing into the now-vacated German positions.

The sun was just breaking through the dense clouds as David and his flight started to land at St. Pol. Brooks was the last plane down and as he came to a halt, Aubrey ran over and helped him out of his Snipe.

"Quite a show, quite a show!" Aubrey said to David. "Good to see you back, dear fellow."

The two pilots started to walk away from the flight line. David smiled at Aubrey, slapped him on his back as he pulled off his goggles, exposing the oil-smeared area around the goggles.

"You seem to be shy two of your brood, David," Jim said, as David looked at his Camels to see who was missing.

"Be a good friend, Jim, take the rest of the flight over to the cantina. There's one of my new flight sergeants standing with his head down." James waved the others to follow him while David walked over to the sergeant.

Noticing tears in the sergeant's eyes, David put his arm on the pilot's shoulder, patted him softly and said, "A rotten business, this! You performed well sergeant. Forgive me, but I can't recall your name."

"It's Johnson, sir, Flight Sgt. Johnson."

"I see," Brooks said, "Was the other chap a friend of yours?"

"Yes, sir, he was; we went through all our flight training together, we were both from the same home town. It's funny, sir, but his father was our local minister, and he wanted so much to follow in his father's foot steps."

David put his arm under the sergeant's and started to lead him toward the cantina.

"Sometimes, Sergeant, I think there has to be a place where people can forever stroll in the sunshine, listen to the birds singing, think of pretty girls and know only peace and tranquility. I like to think that your friend is there now, and that someday we'll all meet there and never know from war again."

As they were about to enter the cantina, a lorry pulled up and out jumped Myles, arm in a sling, twisting his mustache. "Bloody good show, eh what?" Myles said through his big grin.

"My God, Myles, what happened?" David asked, pointing to the sling.

"Nothing much, Leftenant," Myles said. "Just a bit of a nick, from a Jerry Spandau."

"How do you feel, Myles?"

"Fine, dear friend, chipper as ever. I say—what happened to your flight up there?"

David told Myles what had happened to the new luckless pilot. Myles turned to Flight Sergeant Johnson and said, "Rotten luck, old man, Terribly sorry."

The three entered the cantina to the tinny sound of "It's a long way to Tipperary." The strong smell of smoke and the aroma of whiskey pervaded the room. Many of the pilots stood around the piano, singing loud, and thanking heaven, that they had survived another day.

Willie reared his head as if to brush off a fly. "Sleepy head, it's time to wake up, you have been sleeping almost the entire morning!" Liesel said as she pulled back the goosedown quilt. Willie grabbed her, pulled her into bed and kissed her full on her lips. "Not before breakfast," she said, blushing as she gently pushed away from Willie's grasp.

She helped Willie get out of bed, as a knock on the door revealed the presence of Franz.

"Good morning, Herr Leutnant," Franz said, as he began to pull the drapes open. "I trust you slept well."

"Ja, Franz, thank you. I feel like having a bath this morning; could you be so kind as to help me?"

Liesel turned to them both and, smiling, she said, "I'll leave you men to your ablutions. By the way, my darling, Father made me promise I would take you to visit the Flieger Shule here."

"Where is the General?" Willie asked Liesel.

"He was ordered back to Ulm, early this morning, I hope nothing is wrong," Liesel said with a worried look on her face.

"I'm sure it's nothing, dear, you know how the brass is! They're afraid to make any decisions without the leader there. General Eck is a great leader and they need him there for some important planning." She smiled at Willie, and closed the door behind her as she left.

The breakfast of fresh eggs, ham, potatoes and hot rolls was a treat Willie had not enjoyed for a very long time.

The ride to the flying school was pleasant and not very long. On the way, Willie found no signs of a war; everything was so peaceful. The only sight to remind him of combat was that every man he saw was wearing a uniform.

As they approached Oberschliesheim Air Station, they passed the hunting lodge of Maximillian. The sound of aircraft engines running made Willie look out of the car toward the Air Station. The guard at the entrance, seeing the Eck sedan, saluted them and flagged the driver through.

As they pulled in front of the main building, a major and two sentries came up to the sedan. A sentry opened the back door to help Liesel out. The major, seeing Willie with a cane, helped him out of the car.

"Welcome, Herr Leutnant, and as always, Frauline Eck! It is good to see you again."

Liesel introduced Major Ritter to Willie. "Ah, I see you have seen much combat, Herr Leutnant," Major Ritter said, as he steered them to the classroom inside. The students, on seeing the major and his guests, snapped to attention and remained so until the major had them sit down.

"Gentlemen, Leutnant Schroeder is one of the Fatherland's heroes! His medals and his wound speak for themselves. Perhaps one day, some of you will emulate this fine officer. I'm sure he will be happy to answer some of your questions."

After a lengthy question period, Major Ritter interrupted. "Gentlemen, I'm sure the Leutnant is tired, and standing with a cane has not been easy for him."

The Major thanked them both and led them out to their waiting car. Kurt helped Willie into the car, as Major Ritter helped Liesel into the car through the other door. They waved goodbye to the major as they passed through the main gate. The guard at the gate saluted Willie as they drove through.

As they passed Maximillan's hunting lodge, Willie said to Liesel, "They certainly know how to live, don't they, sweetheart?"

Liesel tucked her arm under Willie's and leaned her head on his shoulder as they rode out into the countryside.

The men of 131 Squadron were happy to be back at their home base at St. Pierre. They were greeted by Major Crawford as they climbed out of their planes. When the men had gathered around the major, he smiled at all of them, and said, "Well done! Good show, good show."

As they walked toward the cantina, the major turned to Myles and David, speaking loud enough for all to hear. "Headquarters called before you returned and has confirmed your tenth victory, Myles, and yours also, David. Congratulations to you both."

The Major led them to the cantina, ordered drinks for all and raised a toast to Myles and David. Captain Edwards came in with an official looking envelope bearing the seal of the crown. He handed Major Crawford a letter, which had been delivered by a courier.

Crawford slipped away from the men to read the formal message in private. As he did, a smile broke out on his face. He turned to the men and called out loud, "May I please have your attention?"

Turning to a sentry nearby, he said, "Sergeant, would you have as many men who are outside come in here at once? Thank you."

The entire cantina was bewildered. What could this be? Is the war about to be over?

When most of the Squadron was inside, Major Crawford had the men stand easy as he held up the letter and began to read:

> From his Majesty's secretary: The crown wishes to bestow upon the men of Squadron 131, the Royal Order of Gallantry, for their dedicated service to crown and country. It is this sort of selfless sacrifice that will gain for England the inevitable victory. You men exemplify the courage, tradition and spirit, that has made our England the greatest country on earth.
>
> May God bless you all, and may we soon see peace in all the world.
>
> Signed,
His Royal Majesty,
King George V

A roar went up that caused every man in the station to come running. The door burst open as the rest of the squadron tried to push into the already cramped cantina. When the noise subsided, the Major continued to read. "Gentlemen, you are to stand to, this Sunday, for a formal review by his Majesty's representative, Sir Percival Sydenham, at ten A.M. sharp."

As the men emptied out of the cantina, Myles strolled over to David, put a drink in his hand and said, "Where would I be, old chap, if I didn't have you to add a little spice to this drab existence?"

They both laughed and walked out into the cool fall air.

Later in the day, the major called in all his staff officers and informed them that the battle had enabled the Allies to gain the ground necessary in order to launch a future advance.

With the news now positive, Major Crawford asked David and Myles to remain behind. He reached into his desk and offered them cigars, as he told them both to move their chairs closer to his desk. "I've brought you both in here," Crawford began, "to give you some good news. Leftenant Brooks, as of today, you are hereby, Captain Brooks. As you both know, Captain Edwards will leave after this Sunday for Command Headquarters." David grinned from ear to ear as Myles clapped him on his back.

"Captain, as you know," the major said, smiling at David. "Myles here is senior Captain. I did offer the position of second in command to him, but he declined. He seems to feel you are better suited for this position and I am inclined to agree with him." David turned to Myles. "Why, you old reprobate! I should have known."

"Sorry, Major." David said. "I am actually overwhelmed, I would be honored, Sir."

Myles turned to David and said, "You bloody well deserve it, old man! Good luck, David."

"By the way, gentlemen," the Major said, "you both will receive the Victoria Cross at this Sunday's review. My heartiest congratulations to you both."

"Myles, would you be good enough?" the Major requested. Myles understood and saluted the Major. Turning to David he said, "The drinks are on me, Captain!" David grinned at Myles and sat down.

Crawford reached into his desk, brought out a pair of Captain's insignia. Reaching across, he handed them to David. "I'd like you to have these, Captain, I look forward to having you by my side."

David stood up, reached across the desk and grasped Crawford's hand firmly. "I can never begin to thank you, sir, not just for this great honor, but even more so, for having been my friend. Thank you, sir."

Major Crawford looked down at his desk. Then, raising his eyes to David he said, "Captain, after Sunday's festivities, you and Leftenant Aubrey are to report to Dunkirk Air Station to pick up two new Sopwith Snipes. I could have had them flown in here, but you two have not had any leave for much too long a time, so you both are being given a week's leave in Dunkirk, besides I hear they have some lovely nurses at the hospital there. Do have a good time!"

David took a deep breath. "My cup runneth over, sir!"

"Nonsense, my boy," the Major said. "You both deserve it. I would have sent Myles with you, but his wound has to be attended to, so he will rest here and help me until you return. I'll see you both before you leave. Now run along, Captain, and tell Leftenant Aubrey the good news, I know he'll enjoy hearing it from you."

As David stood up to leave, he said, "You know, sir, I'm sorry I couldn't bring all my flight home."

"Someday, Captain, when you have your own squadron, you will understand the constant pain, to have to sit and write letters of condolence to families and loved ones, and tell them, their son is not coming home. Let's hope, David, this blasted war will end soon!"

David walked out into the cool fall air, took a deep breath and thought to himself, *It's so damned good to be alive!*

Liesel and Willie returned late for dinner. Frau Eck greeted them and handed Willie a letter which had arrived while they were out. "Wilhelm, this came by special messenger," she said.

"Danke, Frau Eck," Willie said, as he sidled off to read the contents.

After he finished reading, Willie looked at everyone with a glow on his face. "It seems I have been promoted to Oberleutnant! However, I must return at once to my Staffel."

Frau Eck congratulated Willie on his promotion, but Liesel broke down in tears.

"Willie, how can they call you back so soon? You can't even walk without your cane! How will you be able to fly?" she continued.

"Don't cry, Liebschen mein, Hauptmann Kruger wants me to assist him in running the Staffel—so you see, dear, I still won't be doing any flying."

Frau Eck put her arms around Liesel and Willie. "Someday soon, this terrible war will be over; the Fatherland will have a great victory, and you both will be married and have many wonderful children."

"Mutti, Mutti," Liesel said, "how I've dreamed of that day!"

The maid interrupted quietly to announce that dinner was ready.

Dinner was a quiet affair; very little was said but Waldy sensed that something was amiss. "Is everything well with Leutnant Schroeder, Mutti?"

"He is now an Oberleutnant, Walther, but he must leave tomorrow to return to his Staffel."

"Congratulations, Herr Oberleutnant!" Waldy said, "But I shall miss you very much. I can't wait to tell my friends about your promotion."

"Frau Eck, I wonder if I can have Franz help me pack?"

"Of course, Wilhelm, I'll get him right away."

"I'll help you also, darling," Liesel added, as she went over to Willie.

Franz came at once to Frau Eck. "You called for me, madam?" Franz asked.

"Yes, Franz, would you get Oberleutnant Schroeder's koffers and help him pack? Unfortunately, he must leave us tomorrow morning."

"Jawohl, Madam, I'll get them right away."

Liesel took Willie by the hand and they both went upstairs to his room.

As Franz laid the suitcases on the bed and began to pack, Willie said to him, "Franz, you have been a good friend. Thank you for your many kindnesses."

"It was my pleasure. Herr Oberleutnant, I hope some day soon, you will come back to stay with us for good."

Liesel, standing near the door, heard Franz's voice, came over to him and kissed him on his cheek.

"You have always been so dear to us Franz! We love you like family."

Franz took the packed suitcases to the head of the stairs and called down to Eric, to come pick them up and put them near the door. He excused himself, and closed the door after him as he left the room.

"Come, Liebschen," Willie motioned to Liesel. "Sit by me here," he said, motioning toward the bed. "It has been a wonderful time for me here, for these few weeks I actually forgot about the war. I shall remember these days and they will keep me company until I return. Until that day, Liebschen, you must be brave and have faith. Now I think I'd better get a little sleep, dear, I must get up and leave early."

Willie pulled Liesel tight to him and whispered into her ear, "What wouldn't I give to have you sleep with me this night!"

Liesel blushed and without looking at him she said, "I have wanted to so many times, my love!" Willie kissed her and as she rose to leave, he said, "Next time, my dearest, you will never leave our bed, or sleep alone."

Willie rose early, washed and dressed with Franz's help. When he came down the stairs Frau Eck insisted he eat a good breakfast before departing. All the servants stood nearby to wish Willie a safe trip and a speedy return. Young Walther ran over to Willie, embraced him and said, "Shoot down many enemy planes, Onkel Wilhelm," as a few tears seemed to creep onto his young face. Liesel, standing by the car, wrapped a long scarf around Willie's neck.

"Promise me you'll wear this around all those pretty girls to remind you, you are spoken for!"

As soon as they were in Willie's room, Liesel hugged Willie, sobbing. "I love you so much, darling! Please come back to me."

Willie held her close, kissing her tears away. "Don't worry, Liebschen mein, I'll come back! I'm like a bad penny; I always turn up."

Liesel smiled through her tears. "You are not a bad penny, you are the dearest man on earth."

When they were finished packing, Willie turned to Franz, shaking his hand and said, "Franz, you have been a good friend! Thank you for your help and care, I shall miss you, my dear friend."

Franz was taken by surprise. "I shall miss you, Herr Oberleutnant, and I shall light a candle for you every day."

"Thank you, Franz, thank you!" Liesel came over to Franz and kissed him on the cheek.

Frau Eck knocked politely on the door and said, "May I come in?"

"Of course, Frau Eck, please!" Willie said, walking over to her. "Frau Eck, how can I thank you for your many kindnesses and hospitality? I hope I did not create too many problems for you and everyone here."

As Frau Eck prepared to leave, she said to Wilhelm, "I will have a good breakfast for you before you leave."

Frau Eck came over to Willie, kissed him on his cheek, turned and left the room so that no one could see the tears beginning to fill her eyes.

The next morning, after breakfast and the sad goodbyes, Willie sat back in the sedan as Kurt drove out of the Eck estate and headed for Munich. Willie sat and wondered. *Would he ever see Liesel again?*

4

The air at Dunkirk was blustery, cold and damp. David and Jim pulled their collars tight to keep out the cold air. "I say, David, why don't we have a little repast? I'm famished. Afterwards, dear chap, we can have a look at the ladies."

"You know something, James," David said, slapping him on his back, "That's the first good idea you've had in a very long time!"

Aubrey grinned at David as they both started down a long street bordering the sea. "Look," Jim said, as he spotted a bobby talking to a young woman, "Let's ask him where a good place to dine might be? He should know. Pardon me, sir," Jim said as he tipped his cap to the woman. "Do you know a nice place to dine?" "Why, yes," the bobby answered. "Miss Nellie's is just the place you'd be looking for. Just stay on this road, make a right turn at that large lamppost, and it's in the middle of the street on your right."

"Thank you, officer," Jim said, as he apologized to the woman for the interruption.

As they started to enter Miss Nellie's, two military nurses came out of the restaurant. David held the door as the ladies made their exit. The first nurse coming out looked up at David and smiled demurely. In a soft voice she said to him, "Thank you, Captain."

Jim and David, about to enter the restaurant, took one last peek at one of the nurses and David was surprised when the same nurse looked back at him.

"Come, old friend," James said, tugging at David's sleeve. "There's plenty more where they came from."

They gave the waitress their order and as they waited, they looked around the pleasant room. Not far from their table, they noticed a major and five officers just finishing their meal. The major looked at David and Jim and walked over to them, holding a cane and walking with a decided limp.

David and James both stood up as the major approached their table.

"Please, as you were, gentlemen," the major said. "Would you be the chaps from St. Pierre Station?"

"Yes, sir, we are, Major. I'm Captain Brooks and this is Leftenant Aubrey. Would you care to join us?"

The Major smiled at them both. "Perhaps at another time, thank you. Your Major Crawford called, explained you were here to pick up the two new Sopwith Snipes. They should be ready by the time you prepare to leave. In the meantime, do enjoy your stay here. By the way, there's a nice place right down the road called The Coach and Four. It's clean, has a fine view of the sea. You might want to give it a go." David and James stood up, shook the major's outstretched hand, then stepped back and saluted him.

When the major and his party left, Jim turned to David and said, "I say, did you see the decorations on his chest?"

David nodded agreement as he poured James another glass of wine and one for himself. "He must have seen much combat, Jim. I guess due to his wounds they put him out to pasture here."

"This is rather good wine, don't you think? Takes the chill off the damp air," David said as they ate their dinner, staring out of the windows in the direction the two nurses had taken.

"Those two nurses were rather pretty, don't you think, Jim?"

James smiled at David. "Aha, Captain! Methinks you have been taken by that nurse, however, sir, we'd better be getting over to the Coach and Four before there's no vacancies," James said. They were checked in by a kindly older woman who showed them to a spacious room with a high cathedral ceiling, and large bay windows overlooking the angry sea.

By the time they had showered and unpacked, the long ride and the wine had all taken their toll. Both men fell asleep almost as soon as they hit the sheets.

The roar of two low-flying planes coming into the Air Station woke David and Jim with a start. "Good Lord!" David blurted out. "We must be closer to the Station than we imagined."

They each took turns washing up at the w.c. at the end of the hall. This was Sunday and the sun shone brightly as its rays danced off the ocean waves.

"I'm famished," Jim said as he turned to David who was just finishing buttoning his tunic, "How about you?"

"Sounds good, James, let's go. We can go back to Nellie's place, the food seemed good there."

"David, me lad, methinks you're hoping to encounter those nurses again!"

"Tell me, James, my good friend, would that be a crime?" They both laughed as they walked out into the warm sunlight and started for Nellie's place.

With their appetites sated, they both strolled down the road toward the ocean walk. The sound of an organ playing and voices singing a hymn, caused James to slow his pace. Without looking at David he said, "You know, old man, it's been such a long time since I've set foot into a church. What say we go in for just a bit?"

As they walked toward the church, David noticed the weather-beaten houses, the drab look, and then the tall spire sticking up from the church.

They both removed their caps as they quietly walked into the church. They looked around and slid into two empty seats near the rear. Jim picked up a hymnal and began to sing the familiar refrain he had known since childhood while David glanced around the old church. He saw mostly elderly people, some small children and quite a few military uniforms. As the congregation rose for prayer, David spotted five RFC nurses standing together. There, in the middle of the group, was that same nurse who had given him such a warm smile, last night. That feeling in David's heart caused him sudden anguish. *What in God's name is happening to me?* he thought. *Am I behaving like a school kid?* He sat back down and spent the entire time looking over at the lady, but she never turned around.

With the service over, Jim wanted to quickly leave but David pulled him back and whispered to him, "Wait just a moment, Jim, let those nurses come by."

James looked over at them and, spotting the one that had taken David's eye, he understood.

As the RFC nurses walked by them the same girl saw David, put her head slightly down, but when she came abreast of David, she raised her eyes and gave him that same warm shy smile.

Jim saw the exchange of looks and realized that David had been smitten.

David and Jim walked out, and stopped at the head of the stairs to shake the pastor's hand. The pastor looked at their medals and said, "May our Lord Jesus bring you both home safe and sound to your families." Both men paused to thank the pastor for his blessing.

James pulled out his pack, took a cigarette and pretended he didn't have a light. "I say, miss," he said to one of the young nurses, "Would you have a light, by any chance?" She held up the light for James and as she did, her eyes shifted to David. Suddenly, she dropped the match as it burned her finger. "I'm so sorry, miss," James said. "Clumsy of me. I'm truly sorry!"

David wet his handkerchief from the nearby small spigot and wrapped it around her hand. The other nurses let out a whistle and laughed out loud. "It seems chivalry is not dead after all," one said.

James introduced himself to the girls, then introduced David. The girl with the burned finger looked at David and said, "I'm Ann

Hingle. This is Ruth Bottomly," and finished by introducing the others. Jim Aubrey suggested a stroll down by the water. Ann and Ruth agreed but the other girls decided they had better get back to the hospital.

"I see you are both pilots, but not from our base," Ruth said, as she slipped her arm under Jim's and started to walk toward the ocean.

David and Ann walked a little slower so they could just talk. Ann turned toward David's chest and said, "I see you have the Victoria Cross, Captain. You must have seen some hectic times, to say the least. We see so many terrible cases come through here. War is so horrible, don't you think?"

David nodded, and without looking at Ann he said, "There's no such thing as a nice clean war, Ann. It's a filthy business. It saps every country of its finest young men. Yet, Ann, we still must defend our country to preserve our way of life." Ann tightened her grip on David's arm as they walked, but David stopped suddenly, pulling Ann aside.

"Ann, we still have a few days before we must leave, do you think you and Ruth could have dinner with Jim and me tonight?"

Ann peered over at Jim and Ruth. "I don't know Captain," she said. "I'll try, but I don't know if we can get away."

David turned to Ann and said, "Please, Ann, it's David, not Captain!"

She gave him that special smile of hers and said, "Yes, David, yes."

Ann told David they would be at Nellie's place by eight, if they could make it. David looked into Ann's soft blue eyes, and very seriously he said to her, "Ann, I don't know when I have ever wanted to see anyone again as much as I want to see you!"

"Since yesterday, David, when you held the door open for me, I have not stopped thinking about you."

Time seemed to stand still for David and Ann, until Ruth interrupted them to remind Ann, they were due back to the hospital.

As the girls got on the bus back to base, Ann squeezed David's hand and whispered, "I'll try to see you tonight!"

Time never dragged for David as it did this night. Eight came, nine came—but no sign of Ann or Ruth. Finally, James convinced David to eat dinner, and he said, "Perhaps we'll see them on the base tomorrow?"

The base was very large, larger than they both had imagined. It was dotted with many buildings, hangars, maintenance shops, but the largest complex by far, was the hospital facility.

Major Firth explained to them that many wounded cases were brought here and given the best care available.

Major Firth took David and James out to the flight line where over twenty new Sopwith Snipes were lined up. As they walked along the line, Major Firth explained that these planes were slated for those units which sustained heavy losses and also for those units with out-dated aircraft.

Near the end of the line, he pointed to the two Snipes slated for 131 Squadron which David and Aubrey would fly back. "I'll have the mechs finish getting them ready," the Major said, "and I would suggest you flight test them prior to leaving for your base. In the meantime, gentlemen, make yourselves at home on the base. I'll have an orderly take your things to your room for the night."

Later, as David and Jim settled into their room, David turned to Jim and said, "You know, Jim, I've really got to see Ann again!"

"I know, old man, but we really haven't much time," David said.

"Jim, I think I'm going to hop over to the hospital and see if I can find her."

Aubrey, seeing the anguish in David's face, said, "Would you like me to go along?"

"Thanks Jim. Yes, I'd really like that." They both pulled on their warm coats and started toward the hospital complex. It was quite a distance but they were fortunate to be given a lift by a sergeant in a truck who was headed in that direction.

"I was wondering, Sergeant, how would one go about finding someone here?"

"That's quite easy, Captain; I'll drop you at the Headquarters building. As you go in, there's a desk with usually three women, they can locate anyone here."

David thanked the sergeant as they pulled up to the main building.

David approached the desk and apologized for the intrusion; when the nurse turned to help him, he asked if he could see nurse Ann Hingle. "I think you might have missed her, Captain; we just received a call from the docks, it seems a large ship loaded with many wounded just arrived and we're sending a large contingent of doctors, nurses and aids to the ship."

David's head dropped. The nurse, seeing his look of distress, said "Wait one moment, Captain; perhaps she hasn't left yet."

She cranked the telephone and made some inquiries. Then David heard her say to a soldier standing nearby, "Corporal, would you be a good chap and rush the Captain over to the lorry loading area."

"Follow me, Captain, this way," the corporal said.

As they rushed out to the motor bike, Jim asked if he could ride along. "Not much room, Leftenant, but if you don't mind sitting behind me?"

"My pleasure, Corporal, let's be on our way."

They sped to the large hangar where six large lorries were being loaded. David and Jim jumped off the bike and ran toward the lorries. David asked a nurse sitting near the back if Ann Hingle was on the lorry.

"No, I'm sorry, Captain, I don't know which one she's on."

James ran ahead of David and began yelling out loud, "Ann

Hingle! Ann Hingle!" Then a voice answered from one of the lorries, "Here I am."

When Ann poked her head out and saw David, she climbed down from the lorry. She then slowly began to walk toward him, then suddenly she began to run toward David, flinging herself into his arms as David kissed her full on her mouth and smothering her with kisses as he lifted her off the ground, "Oh, David, I love you! I'd have died if I couldn't tell you."

David kept kissing her and as he hugged her, he said, "Ann, Ann darling, I love you too; I know it's crazy, dear, but I know I love you."

The crowd of nurses and everyone who witnessed the incident cheered, clapped and yelled with joy.

A colonel came over, and warned them that time was short, they'd really have to pull out. As Ann climbed back into her lorry she asked David to write her and to please come back to her. Ann sat on the seat nearest the back and as the lorry pulled away she threw kisses at David as she wiped the tears from her eyes.

David and James stood out on the ramp. The cold wind had picked up as they watched the lorries disappear as they left the base.

"Come on, my good friend, we still have a war to fight," Jim said, as they left.

As the car approached the Munich outskirts, Willie again began to see the look of despair on so many faces. Kurt, the chauffeur, noticed the serious look of Willie in the rear view mirror.

"They are hungry, Herr Oberleutnant, tired of this war and with so many men never returning to them."

"Kurt, we are out there, every day, fighting for our Fatherland. We see death every day, but we keep on going, Kurt, we keep on fighting for a greater Germany. Some day, my friend, when we have won this terrible war and we come home victorious, you will see how our people will rally and return to a normal and happy life."

"Jawohl, Herr Oberleutnant, perhaps you are right." Willie looked up at the rear view mirror, hoping that Kurt could not see the doubts crossing his mind.

The Hauptbahnohof, was packed with travelers, most of them in uniform. Kurt took Willie's suitcases and helped him out of the car. As he did so, he looked around for the station master. Spotting him off to the left, Kurt went over to him and gave the stationmaster a letter. He read the very formal letter, looking over his spectacles at Willie, then back to the letter. He gave the letter back to Kurt, then hurried over to Willie. "Please, Herr Oberleutnant, follow me, your car is over here," he said, pointing to two special cars with drapes covering the windows.

"Herr General Von Eck would be most disappointed if you did not use his suite."

"Thank you, Herr station master," Willie said as he followed the station master to the car.

It was plush, with soft velour seats, fine polished wood trim and with all the comforts of the day. Willie said goodbye to Kurt, wished him well and settled into his seat as an escort came over to put his things away in the car.

For a short time, Willie sat alone, feeling a pang of guilt, having just seen so many soldiers jammed into the other plain dilapidated train cars. He stared at the opulence of the car; he thought of the life style of the Eck home with its grounds and servants. He thought of his Liesel, but inwardly was happy that she was not depressed like the people he had seen in Munich.

The knock on his door brought Willie out of his thoughts. "One moment, please," Willie said as he stood up and opened the door.

"Bitte, Herr Oberleutnant, would you care for something to eat?" the attendant asked.

"No, thank you; perhaps something later." Willie sat back down on the upholstered sofa, sank into its deep cushions and thought of his Liesel. Oh, he wished so much to be back in her arms!

Finally, the sound of the train wheels and the lonely ride made him want some company to chat with. Willie straightened his uniform and walked out onto the passageway. He left his car and entered a car full of infantry. A sergeant stood up and offered Willie a seat. At first Willie wanted to refuse, but the expectant look on the tired faces made him change his mind.

"Thank you, Sergeant," Willie said, and sat down next to the soldier.

The soldiers began to crowd around Willie. "What's it like up in the air, Herr Oberleutnant?" one soldier asked.

As Willie started to answer, a porter came into the train. "Herr Ober, please," Willie said, motioning to the porter. "Would you bring me six bottles of your best schnapps?"

The porter looked at the enlisted men and back to Willie. "This is quite irregular, Herr Oberleutnant."

Willie stood up and with a stern look on his face said, "You will be good enough to bring them as soon as you can, yes?" The porter nodded and left at once.

No sooner was he out of the car, when a cheer went up from all the men in the car. Willie looked at the soldiers, saw the decorations on many of them, and turned to answer the soldier who had first asked him the question.

"Corporal, we are fortunate in the air service. We sleep in clean beds and eat reasonably decent food, but so many of us die very soon. You here, you who have to live in the filth and horror of the trenches, are the real heroes."

One of the men said to Willie, "Each time we look up at our planes in the sky, and see them tumble to earth, we are glad we are not up there! I suppose, Oberleutnant, it is the same with all troops."

Willie now began to feel the schnapps; he stood up bracing himself with his cane, and thanked the men for allowing him to join him. They all stood up and saluted Willie, wishing him well. He was overcome by their kindness and, turning to them, he said, "May the Lord in heaven bring you all home to your families and loved ones, safe and sound and in a victorious Fatherland!"

Willie strode out with his cane. As he left the car, he turned and waved to them one last time.

It had been a long day for Willie. With the schnapps taking its toll, Willie fell asleep as soon as he lay down.

A knock on the door woke him. "Yes," Willie said. "Who's there?"

"It's Heinrich, sir, the porter."

"Ah, yes," Willie said, as he wrapped his robe around him and opened his compartment door. "Come in, come in."

Heinrich stepped inside. "I thought you might like some breakfast, Herr Oberleutnant. Here is the menu."

Willie took the menu and as he read it, he asked Heinrich, "How much longer before we reach Cambrai?"

"In about three hours," the porter answered.

Willie ordered something to eat and as Heinrich left, he began to pack his things. After breakfast, Willie shaved and dressed, then sat down by the window, pushed back the drapes and watched the French countryside roll by as they approached Cambrai.

The train came to an abrupt halt outside the station, then, after a short stop, chugged into the main station area.

Willie stepped out onto the platform and had the porter put his suitcases next to him. He looked around for someone to help him. Suddenly he heard the unmistakable voice of Hardy. "Willie! Willie! Over here!"

Hardy ran over to Willie, slapped him on his back and as he

did, he ordered a sergeant to put Willie's bags into the staff car nearby. "Ach du lieber, Wilhelm! You look ten years younger."

"Thank you, Hardy, It's good to be back!"

Willie and Hardy walked back to the car, and Willie thought to himself, *My God, how Hardy seems to have aged in so short a time.*

As they settled into the car and it began to leave the station, Willie said, "Well, Hardy, what's new with the Staffel?"

"I'm afraid I have some very bad news, Wilhelm; Anton was shot down by the English. You know something? It was that same cursed plane with the American flag on its side, like the one that shot you down."

"Ach, Willie! He was to have been married this Christmas."

Willie sat quietly, deeply saddened by the loss of his dear friend.

"It's this rotten war, Hardy, this rotten war," Willie said as Hardy told Willie of the squadron's other losses.

Hardy had the car pull up next to Hauptmann Kruger's office. Hearing the car, Otto came out of his office, headed for the staff car and helped Willie out. He put his arm around Willie and walked with him into the office. "It's good to have you back, Oberleutnant Schroeder," Otto said.

"It's good to be back, Otto," Willie said, shaking Otto's hand.

Otto took out a bottle of wine and two glasses and as he told Willie to sit near his desk, he filled both glasses. "I imagine Hardy told you the sad news about Anton and the others."

Willie nodded as he sipped the wine.

"By the way, Wilhelm, Max Ehrlich was transferred to Command Headquarters. You will take over his position, the difficulties are many, Wilhelm. We need replacements, planes, parts; and the morale has dropped since you left; the air battles are now being fought with large numbers of planes, plus there are many more problems. I don't mean to confound you, Wilhelm, but you can see, your help is imperative."

"I will do my best, Otto," Willie said, as he reached for the bottle to pour a second drink.

"As you know, Wilhelm, our planes are now flying much higher and they are finding problems with the lack of oxygen for the pilots, plus the intense cold. Forgive me Wilhelm, how is your wound? I hope it is much better.

"You seem to be getting around quite well with your cane," Otto said. "Be sure to let the surgeon take another look at it. Ach, I almost forgot, Wilhelm," Otto added as he reached into his desk and pulled out an oblong box. "Here is your Iron Cross, First Class. Oberst Von Ritter brought it while you were in the Krankenhause."

As he spoke, he walked around from behind his desk, stood in front of Willie and pinned the medal on his uniform.

Holding Willie by both shoulders, he said, "Go now, Herr Oberleutnant, your comrades are waiting to greet you!"

Willie stepped back, came to attention and saluted Otto. "How can I ever thank you, Herr Hauptmann? You have been my friend and leader. I hope that I shall be able to live up to your expectations."

"That goes without saying Wilhelm," Otto said as he eased Willie toward the door.

Willie stepped out into the sunlight, looking around at the familiar surroundings and thought to himself, *it's so good to be alive and back at my Staffel.*

Hardy stepped out of the cantina and, spotting Willie he shouted, "Willie! Willie! Come, your comrades are waiting inside." Hardy walked up to Willie, slapped him on his shoulder; then upon seeing the Iron Cross, he touched it and said to Willie, "It's long overdue. Willie! Come inside."

As both men entered, the soldiers in the cantina gathered around Willie to congratulate him. When the drinks had begun to take their toll and the noon patrol removed some of the men, Willie thanked them all and left to return to his room.

Sitting on his bed, he slowly began to unbutton his tunic, when a knock came on the door. Willie opened the door to find Johann standing there smiling.

"Herr Oberleutnant," Johann said, "Hauptmann Kruger gave me these to give to you. I will sew them on for you at once, Herr Oberleutnant."

The rain came down in torrents for three solid days, making the field impossible to use. Many of the pilots grew restless, wanting to get back up into the sky. Others inwardly felt relieved they didn't have to fly. *Perhaps,* they thought, *we have a few more days of life?* The sound of the mail lorry brought all the men on the run to see if there was any mail from family or that certain someone.

The mailman, in his dripping poncho, dragged two huge waterproof bags into the cantina.

With Christmas not very far away, many packages were in the mail bags. David had the bartender bring a hot toddy to the mailman. David first called out the names of those receiving a package. But from time to time, he put some of the packages aside, remembering that the recipients had been killed in action.

With the packages distributed, David opened the letter bag. As he called out the names, he came across a letter to him from Ann, which he slipped into his pocket. Near the bottom of the bag, he pulled out a large envelope addressed to him in his father's familiar writing.

With all the mail distributed, each of the men went to his respective billet, to slowly open his letters and to read and reread each precious word.

David went to his room, locked his door, sat on the end of his bed and began to read Ann's letter. She told David of her feelings from the very first time she saw him. She spoke of the wonder of just walking with him, of their first embrace in his strong arms and confessed that she was hopelessly in love with him. She also admitted that she now prayed every day for his safe return and acknowledged that she looked forward to the day they would be together again.

David read and reread her letter many times before he laid it on his table. He then ripped open the large envelope from home and pulled out the many pages inside. He looked at the familiar script of his mother, then leaning back in his chair, he began to read:

>My Dearest Son:
>
>Father and I were so happy to receive five of your letters. We were worried, not having heard from you, but were gratefully relieved when the letters arrived.
>
>The letters warmed our hearts and allayed some of our fears. We realize, of course, that war has its priorities. We thank heaven you are well. All we pray for, son, is your safe return to us.
>
>In your last letter, David, you asked your father about your birth parents. All these years, we never really addressed this subject. Deep inside, my son, we wanted to spare you any undue pain and, I suppose, from a selfish standpoint, we wanted all your love. Can you forgive us, my son?
>
>As you know, we have never been able to conceive children of our own. You, my son, have given us the happiest and best years of our lives. You continue to be the best son any parents can hope for.
>
>Know, dear, that there is nothing on earth that your father and I would not do for you. Forgive me, son; I know you're anxious to hear from your father sitting here beside me.
>
>I love you so, David, my dearest son.
>
>Hi, Son:
>
>Mother has given you our reasons for being so vague about your past, but you have every right to know, so here is every fact from the very beginning.
>
>Before the war, things in Germany were not good for your parents. Your father was a skilled mechanic and he received an offer here in New York. They came here, took a small apartment near

our grocery store and we soon became good friends. Of course, you know we speak German which made us even closer.

Your parents shopped in our store and over the years we became very close friends. One particularly cold and snowy Christmas, your father, having received a bonus, went into town shopping for gifts for your mother and for you and your twin brother, Wilhelm. As he stepped out into the street to catch a trolley car, a large truck spun around the corner and struck your father, killing him instantly.

Needless to say, son, it was the saddest day in our lives.

Your mother didn't want to be in their apartment alone, so we took her and both of you boys into our home. Having wanted children so badly, this for us was heaven sent. You and Wilhelm became like our own children. Your mother was like our own family to us. One day, your mother received a letter from Germany, from her sister, saying she had married a wealthy business man and invited her and both of you to come back home. As time approached for her to leave, you became very ill, son. Your mother decided to take Wilhelm back to Germany with her, and we would take care of you until you could be sent to her.

We, of course, loving you and Wilhelm like our own, were so happy to do this for her. We took you to the best doctors and eventually, you were cured. Your mother wrote often, as we did also, sending her pictures and letting her know you were well.

Suddenly, the letters seemed to come less frequently. Then, one day we learned that your aunt and her husband had divorced and that your mother and Wilhelm had fallen on hard times.

We pleaded for her to come back here and we sent her money; then we stopped hearing from her.

Your father had purchased a beautiful gold German Imperial Eagle and a gold chain. Before your mother left for Germany, I had the eagle cut into two pieces and put on separate chains.

Before she left, we put one chain around Wilhelm's neck and the other chain around yours. Her wish was that you both would find each other and be close as twin brothers should be. We tried finding your aunt, but to no avail.

I know that this news will be most difficult for you. The

thought of your brother fighting for Germany will leave many questions unanswered.

We can only hope and pray, as your dear mother and I do, that both of you survive this terrible war and that you will both find each other.

Until that day, my dear son, your mother and I send you all our love and prayers.

Bless you, Son
Mother & Dad

David sat back, leaning against the chair cushion, trying to grasp all that his father had revealed to him. He reached into his drawer near the table next to his bed, and pulled out the gold chain with the zig-zag cut Imperial Eagle hanging from it.

As he reread the letter slowly, he sat there rubbing the Eagle continuously. *My God*, he thought, *I could have killed my own brother on one of my strafing raids! How in heaven's name can I now fight this war?* David looked at the Eagle and for the first time in many years he put it around his neck. As he did, he wondered if somewhere, Wilhelm was doing the same thing . . .

The loud rap on his door stirred David out of his thoughts.

"I say, old boy, are you decent?" It was Aubrey's familiar voice as James tried the door knob. David unlocked the door as James came in. Aubrey noticed at once the serious look on his face.

"Not to be nosey, old boy, but is everything well with Ann and your parents?"

As David buttoned his tunic, he handed Aubrey the letter from his parents. Jim sat down on the end of David's bed and began to read.

It seemed, to David, hours before Aubrey looked up after reading the letter. "David, dear friend, I'm so sorry! I had no idea—as I gather—you did not either."

"Jim, how in heaven's name, can I go up there and kill with

hate in my heart—as we all must do—if we are to survive in combat? Do I stop and ask myself before I squeeze the triggers, could the pilot in the Fokker be my brother?"

Jim thought for a moment, then looking David straight in the eye, he said, "David, let me ask you a question. Suppose the pilot in that Fokker is your brother: in a similar situation, would he hesitate to squeeze his triggers?

"I know it's a poor analogy, dear friend," Jim said. "But I feel you must come to terms with this very fast."

Letting his words sink in, Aubrey stood up, went over to David, who was sitting in his chair looking into space, patted him on his shoulder and started for the door.

As Aubrey grasped the door knob, he turned to David. "By the way, my good friend, the schedules have been posted; you and I are up for Dawn Patrol."

David stood up much later, and without any thought, automatically laid his warm one-piece flight suit, his goggles, gloves and scarf across his chair. For a moment, he stared at the letter from his parents. He started to put it into his beside table drawer; then as an afterthought, he pulled on his flight suit, and put the letter in the large pocket. David had no desire for food, but he needed a drink so he pulled on his tunic and went out to the cantina.

As he stood by the bar, working on his second shot, Jeffries came in, looked around and, spotting David, walked over to him.

"Well, Captain, what have you to say for yourself?" For a moment David did not answer him; then he looked up at Myles, gave him a slight smile and said, "What's your pleasure, Myles?" signaling the bartender to get Myles a drink.

"I say, old man, is everything satisfactory with your family?" Myles asked him.

"Yes, they are fine, thank you Myles."

Aubrey, just coming in, saw them both and joined them.

5

Willie entered the canteen. The music from the piano stopped suddenly, as Hardy yelled out "Achtung!" Everyone came to attention. Willie, very embarrassed, looked at Hardy; his face broke into a grin and he said out loud, "See? My dear friend Hardy wants to usurp my new job!"

With that, he came over to Hardy, put his arm around his shoulder and called to Johann to give everyone a drink on the house.

Willie and Hardy leaned against the bar, as Willie eyed the many new faces in the room. "Tell me, Hardy, have they had much combat training yet?"

"Not very much, I'm afraid, Wilhelm. The losses have been heavy; so much so, that at times, I never even got the chance to know their names."

"Hardy, do me a favor; call them over here, I would like to meet them all."

After the introductions were done, Willie asked Hardy to have Bolke, Mueller, Bolle and Jennike come to his billet. Hardy smiled at Willie and said, "Jawohl, Herr Oberleutnant."

Willie left and started for his billet, but then Hauptmann Kruger's voice caught him by surprise. "I'm sorry to interrupt you, Wilhelm, but here are the orders for tomorrow. Have you had a chance to meet the new men yet?"

"Jawohl, Otto," Willie said. "I'm having the senior pilots meet me now to discuss a few things."

"Very good, Wilhelm; we haven't too much spare time."

Willie saluted Otto, turned and continued walking to his quarters. When all the pilots that Willie wanted to see were in his room, he stood in front of them and began to question each man.

"How many abshuss so far," he wanted to know.

Leutnant Bille said he now had seven to his credit; Lt. Belke had four, Karl Jennike who was now a Leutnant, said he had eight kills so far.

Hardy interrupted Willie, "I'm sorry, Willie, I forgot to tell you. Karl was promoted to Leutnant while you were recuperating."

Willie broke out two bottles of schnapps, with glasses and had everyone find a place to sit down. "This meeting is most important, I urge you to listen to every word," Willie said.

"Gentlemen, needless to say, the war has taken a hard turn for us all. Our people on the home front are tired of making so many sacrifices; too many men will never return. The population is starving and the mood is not good. I have just experienced this mood in my travels while recuperating. The loss in men and machines has taken its toll on our resources. Hauptmann Kruger was just informed that despite the losses, the Fatherland has still been able to produce new fighters, with more powerful engines, capable of flying higher than ever, and we will soon get oxygen breathing equipment to help us while flying very high.

"So, liebe Herren, do not become dismayed. We will take back the skies from the enemy and hopefully, soon put an end to this war.

"Starting tomorrow, we will begin to fly in much larger numbers. This will entail added maintenance problems for our already overworked mechanics. I implore you, do not be recipients of enemy fire, but rather, you must be the ones to put many holes in their planes. Make them sustain heavy losses.

"One last note; you must make every effort to give our new men added training to try and increase their chances for survival."

Willie looked around at the many faces in the room. "You didn't think I could be so long-winded, did you?"

Everyone broke out laughing, as Willie raised his schnapps glass. "To our Fatherland, my good comrades!" They all joined him in a drink, throwing their empty glasses into the large fireplace.

Hardy called everyone to attention. "To our new Oberleutnant and his Iron Cross." The men cheered, came over to Willie and wished him well.

Willie stood, leaning on the gold lion's head of his new cane and feeling so proud of the men in his Staffel. For the first time, he began to feel the weight of command. *I hope I'll be up to it,* he thought.

Willie thanked them all and reminded the pilots to pick up their flight orders from the table. "Please, don't forget to get together with your respective flights as soon as possible, and review all that we covered here. Thank you all again."

No sooner had the crowded room emptied out, when there was a knock on the door. Willie opened it and invited Johann to come in.

"Excuse me, Herr Oberleutnant, I just came to remove all the glasses and food and clean up your quarters."

"Thank you, Johann," Willie said. As Johann went about his cleaning, Willie started to unpack his things. As he opened the large case with his clothes in it, there on top was a beautiful picture of Liesel smiling up at him. Willie sat back on his bed, looking at her likeness.

Johann, taking a quick peek, said to Willie, "Ach, Herr Oberleutnant! She is a very beautiful woman."

Without looking up, Willie said, "Yes, she is, Johann, I hope one day I can return to her."

"You will, Herr Oberleutnant, I'm sure of it."

Willie stood up, placed the picture on his night table and went over to Johann, shaking his hand and wishing him a safe return from the war.

Willie had almost finished putting his things in order. On removing the medals from his uniform, he placed them in the drawer; then he spotted the gold half German Imperial Eagle hanging from a chain, lying on the bottom of the drawer.

He stood up, rubbing the Eagle, then went over to the mirror, and slipped the chain over his neck. He stared at it for some time, wondering why the half only, and what this must have meant to his mother. *You bequeathed this to me, Mutti, I will wear it now for all time.*

The knock on the door, and the voices of Hardy and Bolle, caused Willie to open the door and let them in.

"Come, Wilhelm," they said. "Even Oberleutnants have to eat!" Willie smiled as he buttoned his tunic. Looking around once, he turned and left for the dining room with his friends.

The heavy rains stopped during the night. November 27, 1917, found the field at St. Pierre so muddy that Major Crawford suspended all flights until the field was capable of landings and take-offs. For the mechanics, the respite was welcome. It gave them a chance to repair the damaged planes and to be sure they would be ready when needed.

David walked over to the cantina. Most of the pilots were congregated around the bar; some were sitting at tables playing cards and nursing a drink or two.

Major Crawford and captain Jeffries stood leaning against the far corner of the bar conversing. Myles spotted David coming in and called over to him, "I say, old boy, down one of these!" he invited handing David a drink.

"Bloody rotten rain," Myles commented sourly.

"Captain," the major said, "I've just heard from Command. It seems Intelligence has information that there is a large build-up of aircraft and additional anti-aircraft units at the Hun field at Cambrai. They also feel that some of the Jerries' top aces are being brought in. This can only mean one thing; they are planning some sort of major action somewhere along the front."

David took a short sip of his drink, put the glass down and, looking at Myles and the major, he said, "I imagine it's Command's wish that we attack Cambrai preemptively and try to knock out as many of their planes on the ground!"

"That's precisely their plans, David. But I say, gentlemen, this is not the place to discuss this. What say we go to my office, call in some of our top pilots, and try to come up with a workable plan that will get the job done with the least loss of men and planes."

Major Crawford waved to an orderly standing nearby and told him to bring drinks and food to his office.

They all were relaxed, the major stood up and unveiled a large map showing Cambrai. The conference began to formulate a tentative plan.

"Before we get into logistics," the major said, "I have some additional information. French units will attack fields away from Cambrai; that could put additional German units at Cambrai's disposal. A flight of Bristol F2B's will come in low, to knock out anti-aircraft positions and take out any targets of opportunity. They will come from 139 Squadron."

"Sounds quite good, Major," Myles spoke up. "But I say, don't you think a large flight like this would scramble everything they have? What have you in mind, Captain?"

"Well, sir, suppose we send in three or four Snipes, at very low altitude, away from Cambrai. Hopefully, they'll send up a small flight to chase them."

The major mulled over Myles' idea. "David," he said, "what are your feelings on Myles' idea?"

"Major, I think it has much merit; it could lull them into thinking this is just a small attempt at knocking out some position, I could take three men and try to pull this off; I think it will work."

Myles interrupted David. "Dear friend, don't you think I can lead this effort?" Myles asked, looking hard at David.

"Myles, I can't think of anyone better qualified, but we need a good leader to take the main effort in over the target."

At this point, Major Crawford interrupted them both.

"Captain Brooks, I would prefer you to lead the main effort while Captain Jeffries pulls off the diversionary flight, then joins you in the attack on Cambrai. Our main assignment is to provide cover for the F2Bs to first do their work, free from interference of other Hun units. In addition, 139 Squadron will use its TF2s to bomb the hangars and any planes parked in the open.

"Myles," the major continued, "pick your men carefully; be sure they have the correct maps. Lastly, Myles, give them a cover story, should any of them be forced down.

"David, I suggest you see Leftenant Phelps, and see how many planes we will have available for this mission."

David nodded and as he stood up, Myles also rose. They started to leave but Major Crawford addressed them. "Captains, I can't think of two finer officers for this very important mission. Godspeed to you both."

The next morning, an orderly awakened Captain Brooks with a message that he was to report at once to Major Crawford's office. David hurriedly pulled on his flight suit and boots and ran over to the major's office. He heard many voices and knocked on the door.

"Come," the major called out to David.

David entered and sat down next to Aubrey and Myles. All the pilots were jammed into the office as the major began.

"Gentlemen, I have just received this from Headquarters, which I want you to hear. A lone F2B was returning yesterday from reconnoitering a sector in cloudy and poor visibility weather.

"Suddenly, the pilot ran into a flight of two Hun observation planes, with a flight of eight Hun Albatross scouts for protection. Captain Mckeever, the pilot, opened fire with his two forward Vickers, sending one of the Hun two-seaters down in flames. The

Albatrosses jumped them from fore and aft. Captain Mckeever sent one down in flames, while the gunner, a sergeant named Powell, sent another Albatross down. Our men climbed into the heavy cloud cover, and were able to return to base safely."

"Hear, hear!" went up in the office.

"By the way," the major continued, "This made eight kills for the gunner. It's action like this, gentlemen, that will gain us the inevitable victory!"

The men all seemed elated as they left the major's office. Aubrey, walking alongside David and Myles, said, "I say, that F2B must be quite a plane. Seems to behave like a fighter! And with a gunner to cover your tail, it must be a blessing."

Myles patted David on the back as he headed for his billet.

"Good luck tomorrow, lads! See you later for a pint or two of bitters."

Aubrey noticed David's expression. "Look, chum," Aubrey said, "Tomorrow the fate of most of the squadron rests in your hands. I know you'll come through for all of us."

David gave Aubrey a weak smile and turned toward his billet. The large knot in his stomach didn't seem to want to go away.

Leutnant Mueller entered the bar amid much noise and smoke. He looked around and, spotting Hauptmann Kruger, he approached him, stepped up to Otto, saluted smartly and said, "Excuse me, Herr Hauptmann, but a courier just brought this and I know you would want to see it at once."

"Thank you, Josef," the major said as he walked away a short distance to read the letter from Headquarters.

Otto shook his head as he read the letter; then turning to Willie, he told him to locate all the senior pilots for an immediate meeting in his office. When the last of the pilots were seated, Otto had a sentry stand guard outside the door with instructions not to let anyone in.

"Gentlemen, Intelligence has confirmed a strong build-up of

enemy planes on the enemy air fields at Vert Galent, Cachy and at Bertangles. They also conform that there is no extra activity on the front lines. In fact, the British seem to be consolidating their recent gains. We are not sure what they are up to at this stage, but we cannot afford to be unprepared. I have, therefore, ordered additional anti-aircraft crews to reinforce those we now have, and we are to receive six new Fokker DVIIs with the new more powerful engines. They will be flown in by six new fledglings from Schwerin Fliegershule and will become part of our Staffel. I must remind you, these men haven't any combat experience and you must do everything you can to try and prepare them. Too many of our recent losses have been these new unprepared young men.

"Now, for the last part of this message," Otto added, looking at all the faces in his room. "Oberst Von Ritter, General Schmoelz's aide, will arrive tomorrow morning. You are to fall out by nine sharp, in full dress uniform, for a formal review. Why this is called for now, is beyond me," Otto said, smiling. "But as you know, orders are orders. That will be all, gentlemen. Thank you for coming."

Willie called out "Achtung!" as the men came to attention and left the room.

After the pilots left, Otto asked Willie, Hardy and Bolle to remain behind.

"Sit down, please," Hauptmann Kruger insisted. "You are the most seasoned men here, the others look up to you," Otto continued. "This is extremely important now, with the many pressures that are to be placed upon us. The replacements are coming through now with less training than ever before. Do you have any suggestions, gentlemen?"

"Herr Hauptmann, may I suggest that every day one of us take up one or two of the new men and try to give them pointers that will help them last a little longer. I feel, sir, that this will instill them with some much needed confidence; also, we can better evaluate each man."

Hardy chimed in. "As you know, sir, our heaviest losses have been the new men."

Otto thought for a moment, reread the letter, then, as he raised his head and faced the three, he said, "The urgency of this order doesn't leave us much time for training; but you have my permission to schedule training flights, whenever the time permits. Again, thank you for coming, and remember, gentlemen, tomorrow, 9 A.M. sharp." Willie and the others stood up, saluted Otto and left.

Everyone was heading toward the canteen when the sound of aircraft approaching caused them to look up.

A loose gaggle of six new Fokkers were coming in for a landing. Anton watched them and said, "Must be the new planes the Hauptmann mentioned! I hope they don't wreck them on landing."

Oberfeldwebel Heinrich Oster came out on the run toward the planes, yelling at his mechanics and plane handlers, "Mach schnell! Mach schnell!" he kept screaming.

Heinrich walked up alongside Willie. Leaning over he said to him, "Hauptmann Kruger wants you to pick one for yourself and I will have it fitted as you like."

"Thank you, Heinie. Heinie, you make the choice. I'm sure any of them will be fine. Also, I would like one for Hardy, Bolle, Belke and Jenneke."

"Jawohl, Herr Oberleutnant," Oster answered as he raced over to grab the wing tips of one of the new planes while shouting profanities at his crew to get them moving.

Otto, who had come out also at the sound of the incoming planes, walked over to Willie. Tapping him on the back to get his attention, Otto said, "Wilhelm, be sure to tell Heinrich to have the planes lined up properly for the review tomorrow."

"Jawohl, Herr Hauptmann," Willie answered and started for the hangar.

As he relayed the message to Heinrich, the sound of the patrol returning drew all their attention. Otto, looking out of his office window, counted each plane as they came in. With all six safely back, he gave a sigh of relief and thought to himself, *I'll be happy to get rid of those few Pfalzs, they've seen better days.* He sat down, to await the patrol report. It seemed there had been very little activity this day, no enemy planes sighted.

The next day's morning air was damp. The smell of grass, intermingled with the smell of the gas and oil, filled the nostrils.

Jasta 18 planes were lined up, all had been cleaned and groomed for the occasion. Willie walked out to get into the forming formation. As he glanced over toward the flight line, he spotted a new Fokker with his coat of arms painted on its side; and on the top wing, flight leaders' stripes were painted in a fresh white pigment.

He smiled over at Heinrich, nodding a "thank you," as he tapped his aching leg. The sound of the staff car swinging onto the field from the main road caused Otto, who was already in front of his Staffel, to call out. "Achtung! Achtung!" Everyone snapped to rigid attention and remained that way as the official car drew up to a halt in front of the Squadron. The chauffeur jumped out of the car and hurriedly opened the door for the Colonel to get out. Otto stepped forward and saluted, Oberst Von Ritter returned the salute as he stared at the formation. An aide walked behind him, carrying a briefcase.

Oberst Von Ritter faced the formation. After a short pause he addressed the Squadron.

"Gentlemen, it gives me pleasure to be here on behalf of General Schmoelz. The General had hoped to be here himself, but military urgency has prevented him. However, I bring you his best wishes and he told me to be sure to tell each of you that it is men such as you who will gain the victory for our Fatherland. I say to each of you: You are Germany. You are the pride that has been handed down since the founding of our great country."

As the Colonel finished speaking, he looked back at his aide, who immediately opened the briefcase and removed a medal in a box. Von Ritter then stepped forward to Otto, and in a loud clear voice he said, "By the order of Herr General Ernst Schmoelz, you are hereby presented with the order of the Red Eagle. You have shown leadership and dedication to the Fatherland in the highest tradition of the officer corps. As of this date, you are hereby promoted to Major."

Von Ritter stepped close to Otto, and as he pinned the medal on his uniform, he whispered to Otto, "For me, old friend, this is an especially great honor."

Otto thanked his friend the Oberst; stepped back, saluted him, turned and took his position at the head of the Staffel.

Pilots who had earned the second and first class Iron Crosses, were now presented with their medals. When the ceremony was over, Otto invited the Oberst and his aid to lunch in the dining room.

As the formation was dismissed, the men gathered around the recipients to look at the medals and to congratulate them. While Otto walked with the colonel toward the dining room. Von Ritter turned to Otto and told him the sight of the planes lined up was very impressive.

"Thank you, Herr Oberst," Otto said. "But we still have some antiquated planes which have outlived their use."

Von Ritter noticed the new Fokker with a coat of arms and flight leaders' stripes painted on its wings.

"Whose Fokker is that one, Otto?" the Oberst asked.

"Why that one belongs to Oberleutnant Schroeder, Herr Oberst."

"Ach, yes! I recall now, he's the young man who was recuperating from a wound when I was here last. Tell me, my good friend, do you think this Schroeder has leadership qualities?"

"He is one of our best, Herr Oberst," Otto answered. "He constantly shows his natural ability to lead and is highly respected by all the men. He is a born leader."

"Good, good, Otto," Von Ritter said. "They are thinking of

forming new Jastas and if Schroeder continues to perform as you say, perhaps one day he'll have a Staffel of his own when you move up."

As they both walked into the dining room, Willie, who had been watching the beaming face of Otto, was very happy for his friend and mentor.

Willie and Hardy walked toward the dining room; then Hardy turned to Willie and said, "You know something, Willie; I miss our friend Anton."

"Ja, Hardy, there is never a day that goes by, that I don't think about him."

Willie thought to himself, *I must write my Liesel; who knows if we will have much time soon?*

Seeing Kruger standing over Oberst Von Ritter, Willie walked up to Otto, saluted him and said, "Congratulations, Herr Major! This is a great day for the Staffel."

Otto thanked Willie as the Oberst looked at Willie and said, "I've heard some very nice things about you, Herr Oberleutnant; keep up the fine work."

Willie was taken aback, beaming, he thanked the Oberst, came to full attention, saluted, turned and went to his table to join Hardy and Bolle.

"Willie," Hardy said, "one of these days you will be a major and have your own Staffel."

"Hardy, my dear friend, I hope this rotten war doesn't last that long."

Bolle and Hardy chimed in, "Jawohl, Herr Oberleutnant; Jawohl."

"Halse und bein bruch," Hardy said. They all laughed and sat down to eat.

The first light snow of this December, 1917, blanketed the field at Bertincourt. With the snow and Christmas almost here, the men began to think of home and all that Christmas meant to them.

In the cantina, one of the men sat at the upright piano, letting his fingers run over the keys, and began to play *Silent Night.* Soon, some of the men sauntered over to the piano and began to sing.

Outside, the mechanics and plane handlers, the armourers, worked feverishly to get the planes ready for the mission. The Bristil F2Bs were fitted with sixty-five pound bombs. The same load was placed under the wings of the Sopwith TF2s. The Camels and Snipes were fitted with incendiary bombs, and a full load of Vicker ammo was loaded into each plane.

Most pilots checked each round of ammo to see that they were aligned, so as to avoid any stoppages. When they were satisfied their plane was in perfect shape, some went to their billets and wrote letters marked, IN THE EVENT THAT I DO NOT RETURN.

David stood by the window, looking out at the fine snow drifting down. *How serene it is, how quiet, it almost makes me forget this miserable war,* he thought.

David started to pull on his heavy flight suit, but then he remembered he hadn't shown the major his report. He pulled off his suit, put on his jacket, grabbed the report and went over to Major Crawford's office.

"Come," Major Crawford's voice boomed at David's knock. Looking up from his desk, Major Crawford said, "Come in, my boy, sit down there. Would you care for a cup of hot tea?"

"Yes, thank you, sir," David said as he sank into the well-worn leather chair next to the major's desk.

David opened the report folder, came around behind the major, and spread the report out in front of him. David explained what each column indicated: plane status, pilot assigned to it, flight leader, etc.

"Looks good to me, David; seems we have almost total aircraft available for this mission. Splendid!"

Major Crawford handed the report back to David. "By the way, Captain," he said, "I contacted our French friends over at Spa 19. Their C.O. is due here shortly."

"Major, I was wondering if you had any late weather reports?"

"Yes, I have, David; GHQ seems to feel this snow is only a light dusting and should stop soon.""

"If it is only a light dusting, Major, it could help increase our chances to catch them with their britches down."

Major Crawford grinned as David saluted him and left the office. The major looked after him and thought, *If only we had a dozen like him.*

Jeffries, Aubrey and some of the newer pilots stood around the bar nursing drinks. Myles, busy twisting his handlebar mustache, spotted David coming in. "Here, Captain, old man," Myles blurted out. "Come have a pint," as he turned to the bartender to bring David a drink.

"By the way, Myles, old man, the C.O. wants us to stand by for a chat with our French friends. Major Crawford mentioned that they have suffered many losses from the Huns at Cambrai, and there's a sort of vendetta brewing among their pilots."

An orderly came in and informed Myles and David to report at once to the major. As they approached his office, they saw the Citroen parked outside. The French chauffeur saluted them as they walked by.

The meeting was short but very informative and cordial. As the French major turned to leave, he told them all that they were invited to a Christmas party at the airdrome. As David walked back to his billet, he was happy to see that the snow had stopped and the sky seemed to be clearing.

Thoughts of Ann crept into David's mind. *If only Ann and I could celebrate the holiday together, how fantastic that would be! Damn,* he thought, *I miss her so much!* The sound of many planes being pre-flighted snapped him back to reality. There was still a war to be fought. Then, inevitably, *where can my brother be? Does he even know I exist?*

David sat down on the edge of his bed, pulled off his wet

clothing and climbed into a hot bath. He sat there for some time, thinking how often he had tempted fate. *You can beat it a thousand times,* he thought, *but it only takes that one time, when the odds are against you.* He thought of Ann; *How little time they had really together. It's funny—here again fate stepped in and in less time than it takes to tell, I met the one girl of all my dreams!*

He arose, dried himself, and started to dress for the mission. Before he pulled on his flight suit, he decided to write Ann and his parents. So many times he had started a letter with the words "IN THE EVENT I DO NOT RETURN"—but each time he had changed his mind.

He first wrote his parents, telling them of his promotion. He spoke as lightly as he could, to allay their fears. He thanked them for the devotion and love they had shown him all these years. David added that his love for them could not have been any greater, had they been his blood parents. To his father, he told him about receiving the Victoria Cross; he knew how proud that would make him.

Having written his mother and father, he took a clean sheet of paper and began to write Ann. He started to tell her that if he should not return, not to mourn him, but because of his love for her, to make a good life for herself. As he reread the letter, he tore it up and started all over again, as though he were going to see her next week.

When his letters were finished and ready to be posted, he put them aside and began to dress for the mission. He put on his long underwear, and pulled the heavy flight suit over his uniform. He checked the large pocket with the letter from his parents, and just for luck, he reached inside his uniform and rubbed the half golden Eagle one last time.

6

Major Kruger walked out on the field with Willie in tow to inspect the newly placed anti-aircraft gun emplacements.

Leutnant Feiler, the officer in charge of the gun crews, walked up to Major Kruger, saluted him and began to walk with them, explaining how he maximized the cross fire positions. Major Kruger thanked Feiler and started to return to his office. As they walked away, Willie turned to Kruger and said, "These new guns are good for high-flying planes, but I don't see enough heavy machine guns for low-strafing planes."

"Herr Oberleutnant," the major said, "You seem to be very sure we will be attacked here," smiling in a joking fashion as they walked. "I think, Wilhelm, with our early warning system in place, should they try such an attack, we would have ample time to scramble our planes." "Perhaps you are right, Herr Major. I think I'll have a look at my new Fokker."

Willie walked up behind Heinrich who was busy showing an artist how to paint an insignia on Hardy's new Fokker. Catching him by surprise, Heinrich spun around and apologized for not seeing him sooner. "Please Heinie, don't let me disturb you, my plane looks just great, I think I'll hop into the cockpit, run her up and see how she sounds."

"Jawohl, Herr Oberleutnant," Heinrich said, waving to two plane handlers to go with Willie to help him start his plane.

Willie sat in his new DVII, listening to the engine. He suddenly had a strong urge to take off and put it through its paces.

However, the dull pain in his leg, reminded him he was not quite ready to take her up.

He climbed down, with help from a mechanic, and started across the field to the cantina. The sound of a single plane coming in caused everyone to look up at the Halberstadt CII trying to land. The pilot seemed to be weaving from side to side. Suddenly, the plane dropped down, hitting very hard and ground looped, coming to a dead stop. Willie and the men nearby rushed toward the crippled plane. Willie noticed the bullet holes along the plane's body.

The alert crew reached the plane first. Seeing that the pilot was severely wounded, they eased him out of the cockpit and rushed him to the infirmary. Willie helped the observer out of the rear seat, pushing the Parabelum machine gun out of the way.

Willie noticed some blood on the observer's tunic. "Where were you hit, Feldwebel?"

"It's just a flesh wound in my shoulder, Herr Oberleutnant," the sergeant said. "I'm worried about Franz, he took quite a few hits."

Willie had an orderly take the observer over to the infirmary. "See that he's taken good care of," Willie said, "and have them let Major Kruger know something as soon as they can."

Willie walked over to the crippled Halberstadt now sitting in the hangar, where Heinrich was looking it over. Willie examined the many holes in the plane as Major Kruger walked up.

"They must have run into some real trouble, Wilhelm! Come, let's go and see how the pilot is doing," Kruger said as he and Willie walked over to see how the wounded were coming along.

As they walked into the room where the pilot had been taken, they saw the nurse pull a sheet over the pilot's head. "I'm sorry, Herr Major, he lost so much blood, I don't know how he ever made it in."

The doctor came over and told them that the pilot had four bullet holes in him, one very close to his heart.

Willie turned to an orderly nearby. "Be sure to have all his personal belongings brought to the major's office."

They walked into an adjacent room where the Beobachter's shoulder was being bandaged. "How do you feel, Sergeant?"

"Not bad, thank you, Herr Major."

"Please, sir," the sergeant asked Willie, "How is my pilot?"

"I'm sorry sergeant, he did not make it, he lost too much blood. He was a brave officer, it's a shame we couldn't save him," Willie said to the observer. "When you feel up to it, Sergeant, could you come to the major's office?"

"Jawohl, Herr Oberleutnant, I will."

The infirmary ambulance, brought the sergeant to Major Kruger's office. Willie helped the observer sit down in the large leather chair near Kruger's desk and told the orderly to have some food brought to the major's office for the wounded airman.

As the sergeant settled into the chair, he noticed Willie's cane. "I see you have been wounded also, Herr Oberleutnant."

"It was, as you say, Sergeant, just a scratch."

Major Kruger offered the wounded airman a few stiff drinks, and then a cigar.

Major Kruger, seeing the sergeant more relaxed, began to question him.

"I must notify your unit, where were you stationed, and which unit are you with?"

"I'm with the 213th Staffel, stationed at Capy, Herr Major. My commander is Hauptmann Leimbacher."

"Thank you, Sergeant, we'll notify your commander at once. Now tell me Sergeant, what happened?"

"Well, sir, we were four scouts, sent out to reconnoiter the enemy fields near Bertangels and Bertincourt. We had six Albatross scouts for protection. Suddenly, out of the sun, came at least ten or twelve French scouts. Before we knew what hit us, two of our Halberstadts went down, one on fire, the other seemed to have a dead pilot at the controls. Two Albatross scouts were also shot down, but I saw at least two French Spads go down also.

"We tried to climb into a cloud bank, but a Spad jumped on our tail and fired at us, a very long burst. I opened fire and, I think I hit him, but we went into the clouds and I did not see what happened to him.

"It was then I noticed that Franz was badly hit. Your airfield was nearest, so Leutnant Jaeger tried for your field. The rest you know, sir," the sergeant said, as Willie refilled his Schnapps.

Major Kruger thanked the sergeant, told him to get a night's rest, and he would be driven to Capy in the morning.

"Vielen Dank, Herr Major," the sergeant said.

Major Kruger and Willie sat for some time after the sergeant had left. "Well, Wilhelm, what do you think?"

Willie thought for a moment and said, "I don't recall them operating in such large numbers as of late. Something's in the wind, Herr Major, but what?"

"I think you are right, Wilhelm. I'll call Headquarters and see if they have anything new. In the mean time, Wilhelm, see Heinrich and tell him I want at least eight or ten planes kept on ready alert."

"Jawohl, Herr Major," Willie said. "I'll also see Leutnant Feiler and make sure his men are on full alert."

"Splendid, Wilhelm," Major Kruger said, as he reached for the phone to call Headquarters.

As Willie crossed the field to the gun emplacements, he proceeded without the help of his cane—but the stab in his knee made Willie take up the cane and continue to use it. *Perhaps,* he thought, *I should see the surgeon; I must get back into the air!*

When he finished with Feiler, Willie returned to his room and opened his closet to get some warm clothes; the December chill was beginning to penetrate his lighter uniform. He shrugged off the cold, reached for a bottle of schnapps, took two long snorts, and sat on the edge of his bed, looking at Liesel's beautiful face.

Ach, Liebschen, he thought. *If only we were cuddled up in your bedroom right now.*

He had a few hours before dinner; so Willie kicked off his boots and lay down staring at the ceiling. He soon dozed off into a restless nap.

December 7th was a windy day, overcast with patches of fog over the wooded farmlands. The men of 131 Squadron were busy dressing in their warmest clothing. Making sure they had their side arms and all the maps for the mission. Every man left his wallet behind, with only his identification in their pockets.

As they walked over to the mess hall for a hot breakfast, many men dropped off letters at the C.O.'s office, marked "JUST IN CASE."

The many planes were lined up in order of their take off position. The armourers were busy putting the fuses into the bombs now suspended under the wings. Flares were put into the flare racks; the petrol trucks moved from plane to plane, topping off each tank. The machine gun canisters were full and each Vickers had been cleaned and oiled. Leftenant Phelps ran from spot to spot, making a last inspection. Breakfast was prepared especially good this morning, but to some of the younger pilots, the thought of the upcoming action seemed to numb their appetites.

Captain Brooks walked over to Myles as he and the three men to accompany Myles on his diversionary flight headed for their planes. As they walked, they finished buckling their helmets under their chins, some wrapped a warm scarf around their necks to try and keep out the severe cold of the flight.

"Jeffries, you old reprobate, wait one minute, will you?" David called.

Myles turned and halted, giving David his big grin.

"It's time to get this show on the road, old man," Myles said as he continued walking toward his Snipe. David caught up to

Myles, and said, "You old Limey, you! Stay the heck out of Hun fire, will you?"

"Give them hell, Myles, I'm treating when we get back, right?"

Myles looked into David's eyes. "You know, old man, for a Yank you're not a bad chap."

Captain Brooks walked out to his Snipe which was warming up as two plane handlers held the wing tips. David checked once more to be sure everything was in perfect working order. Satisfied, he fastened his flight suit, buttoned his helmet under his chin, checked his goggles for cleanliness, and climbed up into his plane. He settled into the cockpit, checked the ammo cans to see if they were full, then signaled the mechanic to hold down the tail.

David pushed the throttle forward, racing the engine to check the magneto drop. Satisfied that all was in good working order, he eased the throttle back. Major Crawford came up to David's plane and shouted to him, "God speed, Captain! We'll have a couple when you return."

David saluted the major, nodding his head, and smiled at him as he stepped back from the plane.

David looked around and spotted Aubrey, giving him a thumbs up. The F2Bs and the TF2s started rolling down the long field, using every inch of field to become airborne with their heavy bomb loads. The gunners could be seen swinging their twin Lewis guns around on their mounts. The fighters now moved out for take off, leaving the field four abreast.

David moved out into position slowly as the plane handlers ran alongside, holding on to the wing tips. He took one last look, first to the right then to the left. Satisfied that all was well, he raised his right arm high, then brought it down into the take off direction.

The first four planes shot down the field and lifted off together, followed by the second four. When all were airborne, they jockeyed to get into their assigned positions and climbed steadily upward to reach their assigned altitude. Once in position, they looked over at each other and followed their flight leaders toward their targets. The field at Bertincourt, which had been so busy, was now suddenly very quiet. The men on the ground watched until the planes were out of sight. For a moment no one spoke; each man hoped they would all soon return safely.

David climbed to eight thousand feet and leveled off. He took a quick look at his flight and set the course for Cambrai. As they droned on, Brooks spotted Aubrey's flight at a thousand feet below. Off to the left of Aubrey, Goodwin's flight was in position also. David noticed some of the new men trying to hold their position with some difficulty but as time passed by, they seemed to catch on and were holding just fine.

The flight leaders, like all seasoned pilots, were forever scanning the sky in all directions, on a constant lookout for enemy planes. As David scanned upward to his left, he spotted the French formation also headed for Cambrai. The sight of the French made David feel better. *They'll come in handy if the Huns try coming at us from above.* He thought then of the others and wondered how they were doing.

Captain Jeffries and the three planes with him had picked up the railroad tracks and were flying very low to escape being seen by the Germans. Myles scanned every inch of ground as he led his group, trying to remain unseen. Still, Myles knew that soon the Huns would eventually spot them and alert a nearby airfield. *After all,* he thought, *this was part of the plan.* Just as he crossed the Aisen river, Myles spotted a Drachen with surrounding ack-ack guns around it. The balloon was tethered to the ground, having just been pulled down by the ground crew. The crew of the balloon were trying to climb out when Myles and his three planes came at them.

Myles opened up fire, setting the balloon aflame as the others strafed the ground positions and kept on following the tracks away from the burning Drachen.

The officer in charge picked up his field phone and frantically notified the field at Cambrai and some other anti-aircraft positions in the general route of the British planes.

The call at Cambrai brought Willie running on the double without his cane, toward Major Kruger's office. The major gave Willie the coordinates which Willie gave to Hardy as Hardy and six Fokkers started to take off to intercept the English planes.

Once the six Fokkers were airborne, Willie said to Otto, "Herr Major, I'd better hop over to Feiler and be sure he alerts the gun crews. Also, I'll have Heinrich warmup our Fokkers, just in case we need them."

As Willie started out the door, Major Kruger grabbed his arm, "Wilhelm, wait! I'll have Bolle do this; I noticed you running over here with a heavy limp, you'll only slow down your recovery. I need you to see that everything in the Staffel runs well."

Major Kruger put his arm around Willie's, and led him back. Captain Jeffries, realizing that the Germans now had spotted him, started to climb and headed his flight toward Cambrai.

Aubrey was the first to spot the six Fokker DVIIs going after Myles' group. Aubrey fired a short burst to alert his flight, shoved his nose down and started a steep dive toward the Huns.

Back at Cambrai, Leutnant Feiler was in the side car of his motor bike, going from gun position to gun position, alerting each crew.

Willie was sure now that Cambrai was the intended target. He had Major Kruger give the alarm to the nearby fields for assistance. No sooner had Kruger notified them, when the first flight of TF2s and F2Bs came in low over the field, dropping their bombs while the rear machine gunners sprayed any target they could see with a withering fire. Some of the bombs fell wild, missing their intended targets, but others hit a petrol truck, setting it on fire; one bomb hit the main hangar and started a fire which reached to the tent and set off an inferno. The maintenance hangar was also hit, along with some ammunition which set off exploding shells in all directions.

Willie had managed to scramble six Fokkers before the British hit them. Planes from a nearby field were engaging the English in a fierce fight.

David spotted a Fokker lining up on one of his new men. He flipped his Snipe into a sharp right bank, kicking his rudder enough to line up behind the Fokker, and sent off a long burst. The German pilot shoved his nose down to get out of the line of fire, spun around to his left, and attempted to climb back up and get a bead on David's Snipe. As David dove after the Hun, he spotted one of the F2Bs faltering mid-air fall off on its side and dove for the ground.

Unable to see what happened to the Bristol, he went after the German. He caught him for just a moment, trying to get a shot in on a Camel. David fired a quick burst; the pilot started to turn out of his line of fire, but David corrected his aim with his rudder, firing a second burst. Flame started to pour out of the hapless Fokker. David now fired a long burst into the cockpit. The pilot seemed to rear up, then slid into his cockpit as the Fokker rolled over and started its final dive to the ground below.

As David started for another Fokker, he spotted Myles' Sniper latching on a Fokker Triplane. The DRI snapped into a sharp climbing turn, but Myles caught him as he climbed and fired a long burst into the DRIs engine. For a moment the plane seemed to climb but suddenly the propeller stopped turning and the Fokker fell off on its right wing.

The pilot climbed out of the cockpit and jumped clear with his new parachute.

In the meantime, David dived down to survey the German field at Cambrai. At his first look, he saw the wreckage of two F2Bs and a TF2.

As David climbed back up to engage another enemy plane, he was acutely aware of the intense enemy ground fire. Looking at the air battle as he climbed toward the fight, he spotted two Spads going down in flames and a Sopwith Camel trying to shake off a Fokker DVII on its tail. Before David could reach the Fokker, the Snipe started to smoke; then flames began to lick back toward the cockpit. The young English pilot stood up and jumped clear, falling to his death rather than burn alive in his hapless Camel.

David went after the Fokker as the German dived to get out of David's guns.

Seeing the young pilot fall to his death; David wondered, *Why in blazes can't we be issued parachutes like the Germans?*

The Fokker that had downed the young pilot now dived toward his field to escape David's guns. David followed him down finally getting into position behind the Hun, and opened fire with a very long burst raking the German's Fokker. Parts of the Fokker's tail assembly flew back as David moved his control stick down slightly. The bullets tore into the gas tank as the enemy plane burst into fire—then exploded.

David pulled back sharply on his control to climb back up away from the heavy ground fire. David realized that his fuel level must be getting low. As he prepared to fire a flare to attract his flight to reform and return to base, he suddenly felt his plane being picked up and thrown into the sky, as if some giant had simply tossed him around like a toy. His controls became sluggish and he knew that he had been hit by a German anti-aircraft shell.

His engine began to cough, then died down, as the prop stopped turning. All David could do now was look for a place to land.

The only level field in sight was the German airfield they had just bombed.

Fishtailing his Snipe, he kept easing it down, leveling off as he did so. As David's Sopwith Snipe touched down, his plane hit a crater and nosed over. Everything went black for David.

7

The German anti-aircraft crew near the crash site rushed over and pulled David's unconscious body from the plane. Leutnant Feiler called for an ambulance and had the pilot rushed to the infirmary.

Major Kruger with Leutnant Jenneke in tow, walked over to the hospital to see if the fallen English pilot was still alive. Otto told his aide to be sure and get all the papers and personal belongings from the Englisher, and bring them to him.

"Jawohl, Herr Major," Karl said as he entered the infirmary. Karl walked into the room with the drawn curtains and looked at David lying limp on the table.

Karl started at once to take all the papers, letters and everything else he could find from David's belongings.

As the doctor removed the goggles from David's head, and wiped the oil slick from around his eyes, David suddenly groaned and attempted to sit up.

"He must have bumped his head in the crash," the doctor said, as he examined David's arms and legs and vital parts.

Turning to Karl, he said, "For the time being, he seems to be in good shape."

Karl, coming closer now, looked at David as the doctor helped him to sit up, and suddenly said, "I can't believe it! Why, he looks exactly like Oberleutnant Schroeder. It's uncanny. Thank you, Herr Doktor, I must take all these things to the Major."

As Karl left carrying David's personal belongings, he took one more look at the injured pilot, shaking his head in disbelief.

"Ach, yes, Herr Doktor! One more thing," Karl said. "Please

notify Major Kruger as soon as you feel he can interrogate him. Ach, it's unbelievable; two people can look like twins and not even know each other!"

"These things happen, Herr Leutnant; they say that in this world, there is someone who looks like each of us."

"Vielen dank, Herr Doktor," Karl said as he turned and left the infirmary.

Karl ran to the Major's office. As he ran, he noticed the ground crew still putting out the fires and some of the wounded still being attended to. When Karl saw the corpses lying on the ground, covered over until they could be picked up, he said to himself, "Why do we even bother with them? Would the English do the same for us?"

Karl entered Otto's office and laid out all of David's personal things on the desk.

"How is the pilot?" Otto asked. "The Doctor seems to feel he will be alright, Herr Major. Also, Herr Major, he said as soon as he was sure that pilot had no broken bones, he would notify you."

"Thank you, Karl," Major Kruger said.

Willie tapped on Otto's door and came in when Otto said "Come."

"Well, Karl, how is the pilot?"

"He seems to be well, Herr Oberleutnant, but you won't believe this; he looks exactly like you! It is so uncanny, Herr Oberleutnant, I could not believe my eyes."

As Karl spoke, Willie stared at the things on Otto's desk. Suddenly, his heart skipped a beat as he spotted the gold chain with half the German Imperial Eagle hanging from it.

Otto saw Willie turn pale as Willie unbuttoned his tunic and reached under his shirt.

"Wilhelm?" Otto asked.

Without answering Otto, holding David's half Eagle, Willie took out his own half and placed them next to each other. Still dumbfounded, Otto asked Willie again, "What is wrong, Wilhelm? What does this all mean?"

"Excuse me, please, Herr Major; I must go to the infirmary at once. I will explain later, Otto. Please Karl, come with me."

As Willie came to the door of the room where David was sitting, he hesitated, looked at both halves of the Eagle and, taking a deep breath, he entered the room.

As Willie stepped in, the doctor was just finishing checking David. Looking up from David, and turning toward Willie, the doctor was suddenly astounded by the likeness.

Willie stood in front of the doctor and asked, "Do you think he understands German, Herr Doktor?"

David smiled and in perfect German, answered, "Just a little, Herr Oberleutnant."

Willie was surprised and smiled back at David; extending his hand; he asked David if he felt well enough to come with him.

"Jawohl, Herr Oberleutnant, that would be fine," David said, as he stood up and started to button his tunic.

Willie helped David off the gurney as he looked over to the doctor for approval.

"I think he will be fine, Herr Oberleutnant, but he may have a headache for the next few days. Take two of these, Herr Kapitain, every four hours for pain."

"Vielen Dank, Herr Doktor," David said, shaking the doctor's hand.

As they walked outside, the fresh cool air helped to clear David's head. "Come, Herr Kapitain," Willie said. "We'll go to my quarters where you can relax a little from your ordeal."

Willie was thrilled that David spoke perfect German, because Willie's comprehension of English was nil.

"That was quite a show you English put on; we must repay you in kind," Willie said, in German, giving David a big grin. "I believe we have met before, Herr Kapitain. I was shot down by a plane with an American flag painted on its side, like yours."

"Ah yes, Herr Oberleutnant, I recall now, I buzzed your plane as you were pulled out to safety. I'm glad to see you are well! I hope your limp was not my doing!"

Willie nodded. Smiling at David, he said, "It's nothing serious; hopefully, it should mend soon."

As they neared Willie's billet, Hardy came over on the run. Willie then introduced Hardy to David. Hardy just stood there and stared at them both. "Ach du lieber, Wilhelm," Hardy said. "I can't believe it!"

"Would you be so kind, Hardy, have Johann bring some food and wine to my room?"

Hardy, still puzzled about the resemblance between the Englishman and Willie, complied immediately.

Willie sat down on the end of his bed, and offered David a chair. The two men sat facing each other.

After a few moments of awkward silence, neither man sure about how to ask the other the important question, Willie took both halves of the Eagle, put them together and said, "Tell me, Kapitain—how did you obtain your half of this Eagle?"

A knock on the door interrupted them as an orderly brought in some refreshments. As the orderly left, David's mind raced, trying to decide how much to tell the man who sat before him wearing a German uniform.

"Come," Willie said, "have a drink, I'm sure after your ordeal you could use one."

"Thank you," David said, speaking in fluent German. As they started to eat, Willie asked David how he learned to speak such fluent German, and David told Willie that his parents and grandparents often spoke German and that he had taken German as a language in school.

When the food had been consumed, David started to tell Willie as much as he felt he could without compromising any information.

David called Willie, "Wilhelm," which caught Willie by surprise. "Tell me Kapitain, how did you know my name is Wilhelm? Everyone calls me Herr Oberleutnant."

David started to explain. "You see, Herr Oberleutnant, this half belonged to my birth mother." Willie interrupted David. "Please, Kapitain, you can call me Willie and I'll call you David, if you don't mind."

"Thank you, Willie," David said as he took another glass of wine.

David pointed to the letter on Willie's table and said, "If you will read this letter, Wilhelm, it will help you understand who we both are."

Tears began to form in David's eyes, which Willie noticed.

"Willie, I believe we are brothers from the same mother."

Willie's heart began to pound again.

"I'm sorry I never studied English, but please, David, read the letter for me?"

David thought for a second, then suggested to Willie to get someone here to translate for him so he would be sure of the letter's authenticity.

"My commanding officer, Major Kruger, studied in London for three years prior to the war; I'm sure he would be happy to translate this for me."

"That would be fine, Willie! Let's take these over to him."

Willie picked up David's possessions and they both started for Otto's office. David wiped the tears from his eyes before they entered Otto's office.

"Herr Major. This is Captain Brooks; Captain, this is our commanding officer, Major Kruger." David saluted the major and (in perfect German) thanked him for the many kindnesses shown him. Otto was surprised at the fluent German spoken by the English aviator. He smiled and as he pointed to a chair for David to sit in, he said, "As you can see, Captain, we are not the barbarians you English make us out to be!"

When all were seated, Otto looked at them both and said, "It's remarkable, how much you both look alike. You would surely think you were brothers!"

"Bitte, Herr Major, perhaps if you could translate this letter that was in the Captain's possession, it might shed some light on this likeness."

Otto reached over, taking the long letter as he said to Willie, "It's been some time since I have read English, but I still remember much of it; so, let's see what we have here."

Willie and David sat quietly while Major Kruger slowly read the letter to himself. When he had finished, he looked at Willie, then at David and slowly began to translate for Willie.

When Otto finished the translation, he looked up at Willie and said, "It would seem, Wilhelm, that you and David here are in fact twin brothers."

Willie stood up and as he did, David also stood up. They faced each other as though it were for the first time. Willie turned to David, put his arms around David and with tears in his eyes, said, "Brüderlein." Otto, watching the tender scene, became saddened. He knew that David, as an enemy pilot, would have to be sent to a prison camp for the duration and realized what this would do to Wilhelm who had just now found his only living relative.

While David and Willie now spoke to each other, wanting so much to hear what each had to say about their past, Major Kruger cut in on the moment.

"Wilhelm and you, Captain, I know have so much to talk about. Wilhelm, take the Captain to your quarters and spend the day getting to know each other. Captain, it is our custom, that when an enemy pilot is brought to our Staffel, we always honor him at a dinner. This dinner will be a double celebration, and we look forward to having you as our guest. It has been a pleasure for me, Captain, to get to know you. Wilhelm, take the good Captain now, I will see you both later."

Willie put his arm around David's shoulders as they left.

Otto watched them as they walked, like all brothers should together, toward Willie's billet. The smile soon left Otto's face when he remembered what he must do.

Otto called the Intelligence division and told them about the doomed enemy pilot they were harboring. They informed Otto that Intelligence would arrive tomorrow to interrogate David before taking him to a stalag. Otto sat for some time, still holding the phone on the hook, and thought to himself, *what a rotten war this is.*

"Well, Brüderlein," Willie said, "Are you married? Do you have children?"

As David started to answer Willie, his eyes caught the German crosses on all the planes lined up on the flight line—and as much as he had loved finding Willie, caution must prevail, he realized.

"Nein, my Brüdder," David said. "I have met a wonderful young lady, but with this war it seems we may never meet again. Und du, Willie, have you a young lady?" As they entered Willie's quarters, David noticed Liesel's picture on the table by Willie's bed. David picked it up, and looking at her beautiful face said to Willie, "You are right, Brüderlein, she is very pretty. If I were you, I'd marry her right away."

"You have a good eye for beauty, David; it must run in our family."

When they had sat for a while, enjoying a glass of schnapps, David said to Willie, "Tell me, Wilhelm, did our mother ever mention me to you?"

"She never really mentioned you, but our Tante, on a few occasions, hinted that I had a brother somewhere, but she was always so vague!"

"Tell me, Willie, do you have a picture of our mother?"

"Ja, Brüderlein, but it was taken many years ago."

Willie brought out the picture and showed it to David, who stared at it for a long time and once again, tears began to fill David's eyes. Willie watched and soon tears began to show in his eyes also.

David looked at Willie as he handed him back the picture, "You know, Brüderlein, you look exactly like her." Willie laughed and said, "*Ja du kerl, und du ach.*"

"Tell me, Brüder, how are your parents in New York?"

"They are fine, Willie, I have been very fortunate, they have been to me, all that any son could hope for."

"I'm happy for you, David. I was fortunate also. The Schroeder family took me in and did everything for me that I could ask for."

"What about our father, Willie?"

"The only picture I have of them is home in my room; it is their wedding picture. She never spoke about her life in America, I suppose she didn't want me to know that she had left a brother behind there. She worked so hard, David, and died so young. I remember when she gave me the half Eagle; she said it was precious and to never lose it. I couldn't understand why, but now of course, I do."

"It's funny, Willie," David said. "They say twins take on the same characteristics even when they are apart. Here we are, we look exactly alike, both pilots and we even talk with the same hand gestures." Willie broke out in a loud laugh, as did David.

"Willie, I know I will be sent to a stalag; could you do me this one favor?"

"Just ask, Brüderlein, what is it?" Willie responded, not sure what David had in mind.

"I would like to write some letters to my parents, to my commanding officer, and to Ann, at least they would know I'm alive."

Willie thought for a while, then, looking very seriously at David, he said, "Brüderlein, write your letters; I will see that they are delivered even if I have to fly them myself."

As Willie reached into his desk drawer and brought out some stationery and a pen, David put his arm on Willie's shoulder, thanked him and said, "You know, Wilhelm, my parents will be so surprised that we met; it's like a miracle, an answer to all their prayers."

"Ja, David; while you write, I will also write Liesel and tell her the wonderful news."

As they started to write, Johann knocked on the door, "Herr Oberleutnant, may I come in?"

"Come, Johann," Willie said. "This is my brother, Captain Brooks."

Johann stared from one to the other, unable to believe his eyes.

"Ach, Du lieber, Herr Oberleutnant! It is like looking into a mirror!"

David smiled at Johann and shook his hand, thanking him in perfect German, which brought another look of surprise to Johann's face.

"Would you be so kind, Johann," Willie asked. "Would you clean up the Captain's uniform for him. We are honoring him this evening."

"Jawohl, Herr Oberleutnant. Please would you take off your uniform?"

David started to remove his uniform as Willie threw one of his robes on the bed for David to put on.

When the letters were finished, David left the envelopes unsealed. He knew their contents would have to be looked at closely before they could be delivered to David's airfield. It was still three hours before dinner, so Willie recommended that David lie down and take a nap. When David woke, he saw his cleaned and pressed uniform, hanging from the closet door.

"Well, Brüderlein, it's time to dress and enjoy a special evening."

As Willie and David neared the dining room, they could hear the laughter and chatter of the Staffel. Willie stepped in front of David, opened the door to let David go in first. Major Kruger called out "Achtung," as everyone in the room jumped to their feet and snapped to attention. Willie guided David around the table to the seat of honor next to Major Kruger. David saluted Major Kruger and, turning to the men standing around the table, he said, "Vielen Dank, meine Herren!" The greeting in German from David met with great approval from the entire Staffel.

Major Kruger handed David a glass of champagne. Willie, standing opposite David, raised his glass, as did the entire room. "Meine Kerren," Otto began, "to our honored guest and the brother of our own Wilhelm. Welcome!"

Everyone downed their champagne while commenting on the startling likeness of David and Wilhelm.

Major Kruger leaned over to David and said, "I hope you are feeling much better, Captain, I'm sure you and Wilhelm have had much to talk about."

"Thank you, sir, I am feeling better," said David. "There's so much to catch up on, but for me, it is the highlight of my life, to finally find my brother!"

"I'm sure it is, Captain." Otto turned to Willie and asked him how it feels to find his brother. As Willie answered the major, Otto noticed David looking at a large long shelf of pewter mugs, each with a name engraved on it. Otto turned from Willie and said to David, "Captain, we call them Ehrenbeckers, each one on the shelf is a fallen comrade."

David picked up his glass of champagne, and, still looking at the mugs, raised his glass in a toast.

The men sitting at the table and watching his gesture, now raised their glasses also, and saluted their fallen comrades. After this ritual was concluded and the dinner eaten, the men stood up taking their cigars and cigarettes with them to a hall where an upright piano stood and a long bar.

Major Kruger took David's arm and, nodding to Wilhelm to follow, led them over near the piano. One of the pilots sat down at the piano and began to play popular songs which soon had many of the Staffel singing. David picked up the lyrics as they sang, and joined in the songfest much to the delight of Willie and the others.

David noticed one young pilot staring at him with a look of anger. Willie caught the look, and, leaning over to David, he said "His brother was shot down today by one of your planes."

David walked up to the pilot, offered him a drink and asked if he might salute the memory of a brave pilot. The young officer looked around at his comrades and seeing them nod yes, he took the glass and with David, they toasted his dead brother.

Willie, standing next to Otto, observed the toast. Major Kruger said to Willie, "You know, of course, Wilhelm, tomorrow they're sending a man to interrogate the Captain, and then he will be sent to a Stalag for the duration."

"Yes, I know, Herr Major."

"I was wondering, Otto, could he be sent to a stalag somewhere near Munich or Oberschliesheim? That way, my Liesel could perhaps bring him some fruit or food."

Major Kruger, still watching David, turned to Willie and said, "I will do my best, of course, Wilhelm. He seems like such a nice chap, he could easily fit in here like one of us, Ja?"

"Jawohl, Otto, he could. After all, he's of my blood."

Many of the pilots came over to Willie and David, asking many questions and enjoying their good cigars and wine.

Willie saw David yawn and suggested that perhaps he try and get some rest. They paid their respects to Otto and the men and both walked out, arm in arm to Willie's billet.

As they sat in Willie's room, they talked about tomorrow and promised each other that they would stay in touch. David handed Willie the letters he had written. "Don't worry, Brüderlein, I will see that these letters are delivered."

Major Crawford sat in his office, having just received a citation from Command Headquarters. As yet, he had not received word from the Germans on the fate of the men lost over Cambrai. He thought of David and who could be moved up into his place. Myles would now have to fill the vacancy left by Captain Brooks' promotion.

The knock on the door, snapped the major out of his deep thoughts. "Come," he said. Myles came in and sat down on the old weather-beaten leather chair next to the Major's desk.

"You called, sir?"

"Yes, Myles, you know, of course, you'll have to step into the number two spot now."

Major Crawford carefully watched Myles' expression as he answered, "I imagined that was the reason you called, Sir. I will of course do my best. By the way, Major—has there been any word yet about David and the others?"

"No, I'm sorry to say, we have not had any word. Also, Myles, High Command just confirmed your balloon and two Fokkers. Congratulations. Let me see now, that gives you eleven kills to your credit! Splendid show, Captain."

"Leftenant Goodwin confirms he saw Captain Brooks' damaged Snipe start to land, then flip over. He said he could not see what happened after the crash."

Major Crawford then said, "Captain Brooks' additional kills were also confirmed, giving him thirteen to his credit. Let us hope, he survived the crash and is well."

"I'm not a praying man, Major," Myles said as he started to stand up, "But I'm saying one for him.

"Captain, I need a drink—shall we?"

As they came into the cantina, Aubrey approached them. "Excuse me, Sir," he said, looking at the major. "Is there any word yet on Captain Brooks or the others?"

"I'm afraid not yet, but we should hear something soon. The Germans always notify us as we them."

Aubrey looked over to Myles, "What in God's name shall I write his Ann?"

Major Crawford looked at Jim sternly, "We do nothing, Leftenant, until we have confirmation."

Major Crawford called everyone in the cantina to attention. Putting them at ease, he told them of the congratulations received from High Command. After many "Hear! Hears!" and drinks on the house, Major Crawford excused himself and left for his office, where he sat at his desk looking at the stationery to write the families of the fallen men. He looked back over his shoulder at the large rectangular picture of the original Squadron, and from face to face of each man, so many of them would never go home. As his eyes landed on David's face he thought to himself, *When will this madness ever end?*

It was late in the evening when Phelps, the line officer, knocked on the major's door. Having been invited in, Phelps apologized to the major for the disturbance. "Pardon, Sir, I just thought you would like to know that everything is ready for the dawn patrol. Most of the planes are in decent shape; some have quite a few bullet holes but they should be patched by tomorrow. Two of the Camels received hits in the engines and I am replacing both of them as soon as they come in."

"Thank you, Tom. Here, sit down, have a drink," the major offered as he brought out a bottle of whiskey. "It's been a hectic day for us all, Tom."

"Yes, Major, it has."

"You know, Tom, I've had to sit here and write so many letters to loved ones of families of those brave lads who gave their all; you would think it gets easier, but you know, Tom, it gets more difficult with every letter."

Phelps stood up and as he prepared to leave he said, "Major, sir—I wouldn't have your job! No sir, it's bad enough to see those young faces when we strap them in, looking all excited and trying to act brave, and then they don't come back. No, sir, Major—I wouldn't want your job, sir."

Major Crawford looked up at Tom. "Thank you for coming by, Tom. Well done to you and your splendid crew."

"Thank you, sir," Phelps said as he saluted the major and turned and left. Crawford took the bottle, started to put it back, then looking once again at the Squadron picture, he held up the bottle, and took a long drink.

Five days had passed; still no word of the fallen men. Major Crawford started for his billet looking up at the moon peering down through the broken clouds. The sound of a low flying plane suddenly caught his ears. The anti-aircraft lights shot up into the sky to try and pick up the plane, guns loaded and trying to find the target. The lights caught the sight of a lone Fokker DVII as it shot across the field, very low, just over the tree tops. As it came across, the lights picked up a bundle twirling down with streamers attached. The Fokker remained low so that the gunners could not get a shot at it as it skimmed over the tree tops and disappeared as fast as it came.

Sgt. Caplain was first to reach the bundle. He picked it up and headed for Major Crawford who was walking hastily toward him.

The entire Squadron on hearing the plane came running out to see what it was all about. Everyone knew what the bundle was and they were anxious to hear what information it might bring.

"What say, lads, we all go into the cantina where we have some light and the major can open the bundle," Myles said.

As the major emptied the bundle contents, helmets of crews from the Bristols and the TF2s fell out first. The blood stains were still very vivid and put a solemn look on everyone's face. The identification tags made a clanking sound as two fell on the floor. There were assorted personal effects also in the bundle.

Major Crawford picked up a letter addressed to the commanding officer, which he slowly opened and in a halting voice, read aloud for the group. The letter referred to the lost men as brave heroes who died fighting for their country, and went on to say that they were given a proper funeral with full military honors.

Furthermore, the letter continued, Captain Brooks had survived his crash and was well and that he was being sent to a prison for officers.

Two letters lay on the table, Major Crawford handed over one addressed to Jim Aubrey and the second one, being addressed to him, he put in his tunic.

He would have liked to read it in the privacy of his office but as he opened it, slowly read its contents, he felt it was really for the entire Squadron.

Dear Sir:

I hope that you receive this letter. If you do, it will probably be delivered by my brother! Major Crawford, no one should ever stop believing in miracles. First, sir, I am well and have been treated exceptionally fine. I have been shown the utmost courtesy and have received the best medical attention.

As you know, I had a twin brother whom I never saw, he having grown up in Germany, I in America. When I woke up in the infirmary here after my crash, the face that looked into mine, was that of my own brother Wilhelm. It was like a dream! He is also a pilot and a senior officer with his unit. He limps slightly from a crash. He was my ninth victory, sir, and the limp is due to my victory. It pained me to learn this but he is very understanding.

As I write this, I think of you, sir, and the many wonderful comrades I have known. Major Crawford, I shall miss your calm, your friendship and your constant guiding hand. You have been not only a great leader, but my friend and mentor. Thank you, sir, for the countless kindnesses you have afforded me.

Myles, you old reprobate! I shall miss your wit, your mangy mustache and the courage you have always shown. You are a friend I shall never forget.

Jim, we have shared many close encounters and many good times. I shall miss you also, my dear friend. Lastly, Major, my mind runs back to those brave lads I knew, who have gone West. I am proud to have been a member of Sqd. #131.

The letter went on asking Major Crawford to write to his family and let them know about his brother, and that he is being treated very well. He ended the letter with a prayer that the next year would bring peace and good will, and signed it Captain David Brooks, Royal Flying Corps.

Major Crawford put the personal effects into his briefcase and walked out into the cold night air. As he gazed skyward at the light snow just beginning to fall, a shooting star suddenly lit up the dark sky, and faded away just as soon as it appeared. He thought, as he trudged back to his office, that star is like our lives. *We light up the world such a short time, and fade away just as soon.* He took one last look up at the sky and, spotting the North Star said, "That's for you, Captain David Brooks! May it shine for you always."

Jim Aubrey hurried over to his billet, locked his door, sat down on the edge of his bed, tore open the letter, and began to read.

Jim, my dearest friend, I will really miss you. All my prayers are for you to survive this mess and one day have a large happy family.

Jim, please contact Ann. Tell her I'm well and being treated just fine. Also, Jim, tell her that if I can write, I surely will; if not, please tell her that my every wish is to some day make her Mrs. David Brooks. When this rotten war is over, Jim, I hope we can find each other and stay the wonderful friends we have been. Bless you, my dear friend.

Signed, David

8

December, 1933, was a bitter cold month. David and Ann stood by their car, with the children inside, as they both stared at the gangplank of the *Acquitania* which was unloading at the New York pier.

They began to grow anxious as the passengers poured down, but no sight of Willie and Liesel. Suddenly, David yelled, pulling Ann after him. "There they are, Ann! There they are," David said, first walking, then running toward Willie.

As they neared them, Ann saw Liesel pulling her thin coat tight around her to keep out the cold, while hugging her little girl. For a moment, David and Willie just looked at each other, then with a sudden rush, David grabbed Willie in a bear hug. "Willie! Willie! Brüderlein," David said as he let his joyful tears fall. They embraced each other for what seemed like a very long time, until Willie said to David, "Come, Brüderlein, let me introduce you to my family."

When they both turned to look at the girls and the children, they spotted Liesel and Ann hugging each other and the children.

"Come," David said, "get into the car, it's bitter here." David flagged a porter to put Willie's luggage in the trunk and on the roof rack of his station wagon.

After the children and Ann and Liesel were inside, David started to open the front door for Willie. Suddenly, a flight of U.S. Army Air Corps planes flew by in a Vee formation. Willie stopped, looked up then to David. David smiled at Willie as he started to enter the station wagon. "They say this was the war to end all wars, Willie."

Willie, still staring up at the distant flight, looked at David and said, "Ich hoffe, Brüderlein, Ich hoffe."

9

The year 1933 saw the beginnings of a great Depression all over the world. In Germany, the Weimar Republic was not a success. It helped foster the rise of Adolf Hitler and his Third Reich. The world was just beginning to take notice of him.

David located Ann soon after his release from the Stalag. They were married in a small church near Duxford, England. He brought Ann to America, and took over his parents' business. Despite the economy, his business was able to hold its own. Ann and David had two children, with a third on its way.

The eldest, a son, was named Wilhelm. The second, a girl, was named Sara after David's mother.

David hunted for Wilhelm from the moment he was released from the stalag, but had not been able to find him or Liesel.

Finally, one day, a cable came. It was from Wilhelm. He and Liesel were married and had a little girl named Rozina. They had fallen on hard times but were happy to have found David and Ann. David immediately wired Willie money for them to come to America.

Willie sat, read and reread the cable. The thought of moving to a strange land and learning a new language bothered him greatly. As he sat trying to write David, Liesel put her arms around her husband's neck and pleaded for him to please move to America and to David. "I know how much he loves you, Willie, and I know how much you miss him and love him." Willie touched her hand, looked up into her face. Then, looking back at the cable and the money order, he nodded yes.

Epilogue

July 19th, 1918; Major McCuddin, while on leave in England, was preparing to take off in his new Sopwith SE5, when it crashed, killing him instantly. One of England's greatest air aces, with 56 victories, was gone; still in his twenties.

August, 1918; the greatest ace of the First World War, Baron Manfred Von Richthofen, was shot down and killed after his 80th confirmed kill.

Major Kruger remained in the German Air Service and would later become a general in the newly formed Luftwaffe.

Hardy Buckler went home to Ulm, married a wealthy girl and became an executive with the Daimler Benz Co.

Karl Jenneke joined the Nazi party and became an instructor with the Lufthansa Co.

Oberst Von Ritter would end up on a meat hook at Flensburg prison, having been accused of the plot to kill Hitler.

General Von Eck remained in the service, but died shortly after the war from the flu epidemic.

Walther Eck was finally accepted into the Infantry, and was killed after only two weeks at the front.

Frau Eck gave up her estate and moved in with a maiden aunt near Berlin.

Captain Myles Jeffries was awarded a decoration which was bestowed upon him by King George V, at Buckingham Palace after the armistice. He became a general in the newly formed Royal

Air Force. He never married and still wears his handlebar mustache.

Jim Aubrey married a pretty Irish lass, grew fat and happy and had six children. Their first born son was named David. Jim and David still keep in touch. The other flight members seemed to fade away after the war.